A SUPERNATURAL THRILLER

"War makes monsters of us all."

George R. R. Martin

Prologue

Day One
07:14
Fifty Years Ago

A bead of sweat rolled down Private Tran Duc Nam's face, gathering specks of mud and blood that had dried upon his blistered skin.

The barrel of a revolver pressed into his temple, cold and slick in the damp morning air. *Why me?* the young soldier wondered.

Nam watched the droplet fall and slowly seep into the damp soil between his knees. He raised his eyes towards the man standing before him and had never felt so pathetically powerless. "I have a child," Nam proffered in one last attempt to appeal to his captor's sense of morality.

The voice that replied was cold and straight to the point. "If the tables were turned, would you show me mercy?"

The sergeant was a thickset man, not tall, only an inch more than Nam himself. He had blonde hair and a layer of darker stubble peppered with grey. His sleeves were rolled up to his elbows, revealing a faded pair of crossed swords tattooed on his left forearm. The sergeant wasn't like the other poorly trained young men that Nam had encountered, and in many cases, killed. This man was a professional.

The young soldier sighed. They both knew the answer. "No."

"Ain't that the truth. Now, hands on your head."

Nam did as he was ordered, clasping his eyes shut, trying to focus on the gentle breeze. Although it offered only the slightest relief from the stifling humidity of the forest, anything that could put his mind elsewhere was welcome.

The sergeant pushed the barrel harder and Nam couldn't help but shy away, as much as wanted to greet death with dignity.

"Last chance to talk," the American said. "One way or another, I *will* bring the wrath of God down on this island. Now, whether you live long enough to try and stop me, well, that's up to you."

Nam's thoughts drifted to his family. Would they pray for him if he failed to return? At least that way he wouldn't be just another nameless body missing in action until the leaves covered him and he slowly became one with soil.

He thought about his daughter, recalling the warm summer day she'd come into this world and given his life meaning. If his death was the price of keeping Ly safe, it was one he would gladly pay.

"Kill me."

A deafening roar erupted from the weapon. The sheer volume screamed and twisted in Nam's head, becoming pure agony. Thankfully, a fraction of a second later, darkness overtook the pain, swallowing him like the current of a deep fast-flowing river. Nam died.

For the next hour, the squad of marines argued in the clearing while all traces of Private Nam's warmth evaporated into the thick jungle air. Finally, they left too.

Hours ticked by as the body cooked under the blistering summer sun. Eventually, a rolling wave of black clouds crashed across the sky. With a rumble of thunder and a crack of lightning, they broke.

Thick droplets of summer rain pounded down on Nam's corpse. The deluge washed away the fragments of skull, a mess of grey and white matter, and congealing blood that had once held his consciousness.

To the west, the last rays of a red summer sun emerged briefly from the clouds. They vanished a moment later behind vast, forest-covered peaks that seemed to stretch up to the heavens themselves.

From the moment Nam had been forced to his knees in the clearing, he'd known that this would be his resting place for eternity. Nam was wrong.

Night came and went. The morning sun crept back over the peak of Hill Two Fourteen and swept across the valley. The residual waters turned to vapour, rising in a cloud of white mist that dusted the canopy like powdered sugar.

Sour, stale air filled the dead soldier's lungs. With a grind of bones and a crunch of seized, atrophied limbs, the fingers that had once belonged to Nam pierced the sodden ground and found purchase. Mud sucked his face and chest down, as if refusing to release his body from its death grip. He pushed hard and rose slowly, first to his knees and then to his feet. *Where am I?*

Through the heat of countless summers, windswept autumns, frigid winters, and dank, humid springs, Private Tran Duc Nam rose and fell. Again, and again, and again. His battle eternal.

Chapter One

Day Zero
16:23
Present Day

Hector James skidded to a halt in the driveway, kicking up a cloud of yellow dust.

Ali flicked off his idling bike engine and Hector followed suit. The sudden silence, after the hum and clatter of engines for hours on end, was a drastic change. He'd forgotten how quiet it could be out here.

A thick paste of dust and tears had congealed in the corners of his eyes. Hector wiped them clean. His back was aching and his fingers were stiff, numb from the constant blast of the wind, but also sunburnt at the same time.

Before them stood a pale-blue bungalow that, from the exterior at least, seemed to be nothing more than a single room.

The front of the building was wide open, with a sliding metal shutter pulled across to one side. To the right of the house, a wooden hut on stilts extended out of the ground, reaching up twenty-five feet.

The structure was made of panelled wood slats. It had a triangular thatched roof overhead, and a rough wooden staircase running up one side towards an open doorway. Beneath the first floor was a concreted courtyard-like space, with a pair of khaki net hammocks strung up between two of the supporting pillars.

Having caught the sound of the motorbikes, a woman in her mid-forties stepped out of the house and gave them a wave. She had long, dark hair and maroon tattooed-on eyebrows. This, combined with her white silk pyjamas and a pair of blue rubber flip-flops, made for an odd choice of attire. Even so, she was an attractive woman. *She must have been stunning in her youth.*

"Hello. Mr Hector?" The woman said in a singsong, girly tone. She changed her indoor flip-flops for another pair at the door and made her way over to the bikes, carefully avoiding the potholes in the path.

A sandy coloured dog jogged out behind her and excitedly nipped at one of her heels. The woman hissed and gave the creature a light kick, causing it to flee back towards the house.

"Yes, that's me," Hector said, impressed with her English. They were so far into the Vietnamese countryside that they'd hardly met anyone who knew more than a few words of their language. In fact, he wasn't even certain what country they were in at the moment. They'd been flirting with the border of Laos all day, technically slipping in and out of the tiny nation several times.

"I'm Van," she said, pronouncing it like *Vun* rather than how it was spelled. Almost everyone he'd met in Vietnam seemed to share one of about five different names. This helped with linguistic familiarity but made it extremely confusing to remember what anyone was called.

"*Xin Chao Chi,*" Ali said in his best attempt to nail the tones and correct honorific of the language. It sounded good to Hector, but that wasn't saying much.

"*Xin Chao,*" Van replied, offering him a flirty wink. "Please come inside," she said, flicking back to English, then turned to give the dog that was back sniffing around her ankles another tap.

Hector pulled his camera bag off the home-made steel rack on the rear of his battered Honda Baja 250 and followed their host.

Ali caught his friend's gaze as they walked. "Hot as fuck," the six-foot-four Australian mouthed, bringing a smile to Hector's face. As always, there was only one thing on his mind.

At the doorway, Hector perched on a foot-high ledge in front of the shutters. He pulled off his Doc

Martens and socks, relishing the feeling of air between his toes.

To his right, Ali kicked off a pair of flip-flops. "Take a gander at these piggies," he said, proudly displaying the thick white tan lines contrasted by the seared, red skin on his feet.

Hector winced. "Should've covered up."

The Australian shrugged, pulled out a tube of red pawpaw paste and smeared it carelessly over his feet. "This shit takes the edge off anyway."

Stepping inside, it took a few seconds for Hector's vision to adjust to the darkened room. The house had a musty smell and he fought back a sneeze as the dust tickled his nose. Overhead, a ceiling fan whirred, working in conjunction with the airy design, to create a pleasant sort of natural air conditioning.

The interior had off-white walls and a green-tiled floor that was refreshing beneath Hector's sweaty, now-bare feet. The room was wide but sparse, with a TV mounted to the right of the shutter and a karaoke unit beneath it. A dividing wall ran halfway across the length of space, hiding what Hector guessed must be a couple of small bedrooms. In front of the wall sat a carved wooden sofa and a matching glass-topped coffee table.

Ali strutted in a second later as if he owned the place, adorned in a Hawaiian shirt, denim shorts, and

Bia Hoi vest top. In the few years that had passed since he and Hector had worked together at a beach bar in Brighton, Ali seemed to have somehow become even more outgoing.

Van motioned for them to sit on the wooden sofa beside her. Hector inched between it and the coffee table, noting how needlessly decorative the piece of the furniture was as he went. The arms and backrest of the seat were carved into swirls and symmetrical patterns from a huge, varnished chunk of dark wood. *Could have spent a little longer trying to make it comfortable instead*, he thought, trying to relax on the hard, angular seat.

Ali sat down, pushing the table forward with his knees, creating a terrible scraping sound that was made sharper by the abundance of flat stone surfaces.

"RICKY!" Van screamed towards the back door on the right-hand side of the room. A skinny, twenty-something-year-old, popped out of the doorway a couple of seconds later and walked over, standing beside his mum.

Ricky had big bulging eyes, and a toothy grin that looked too wide for his thin face, the combination of which gave him an insect-like quality.

Like many men of the younger generation Hector had met so far in Vietnam, Ricky dressed in tight jeans and a knock-off designer T-shirt. This particular one was black with sparkly gold lettering on the front. Complementing his choice of outfit was a selection of poorly inked forearm tattoos featuring dragons, misspelled English phrases, and crude *hentai* characters.

"Ah, hey guys," Ricky said in an over-the-top twangy American accent. "You're Hector, the journalist, right? We spoke online."

"Ha!" Ali chipped in. "An aspiring one, maybe."

Hector shot his friend an icy glare, choosing not to counter with the fact that he'd been published a dozen times over the last year. Honestly, he still felt like a fraud being called a journalist but forced himself to do it anyway.

"Thanks, mate," he said and turned back to his hosts. "Nice to meet you."

Ricky nodded in response. "You two can stay here. I'll go grab your bags off the bikes."

He shot off out the front of the house and returned a few seconds later, carrying a pair of hefty backpacks. He dropped them on the floor by the shutters. "I gotta get your room ready, but we'll catch up later, yeah, guys?" he said, as though addressing a pair of old friends.

"Err, yeah sure." Hector nodded.

"You got it, bro," Ali said, giving him a double finger gun gesture and miming pulling the trigger.

Van picked up the white teapot from the centre of the table and poured green tea into a pair of tiny white porcelain cups. She passed one to each of the guests and then slid a plate of stubby, half-brown bananas towards them. "You must be hungry. These are from my garden. No chemicals."

"Thanks," Hector said, picking up one banana and passing another to Ali on his right, who looked at it with the same confused and disgusted expression he might have if someone had just handed him a bag of dog turd.

Van slid up next to Hector, close enough that he could smell the fruity aroma of her perfume.

"Fill this for me," she said, pulling a guest registration document from a shelf below the glass and laying it on his lap. "How long will I have you?"

Hector glanced over at Ali to confirm, even though it was him who had planned the trip out. Hidden from Van's line of sight by his shoulders, Ali responded by rapidly thrusting the mini banana in and out of his mouth, as if performing an act of fellatio on the tiny yellow cock.

Hector bit his lip, trying to stifle a smirk, and failed. "Just one night. We're on a tight schedule."

"He never shuts up about the damn schedule," Ali said with a snort. "You're on holiday, man. Relax."

"It's okay," Van said, looking mildly disappointed. "Can I see your passports?"

The two men both passed her their documents, and without another word, she stood up and walked off with them to a back room. "We'll have dinner at seven," she called back. "It'll be late when the others arrive."

He met Ali's gaze to see his friend looking equally confused. They were literally in the middle of nowhere, and Van couldn't have more than one spare room. *What others?*

Chapter Two

Day Zero
16:48
Present Day

Hector sipped his green tea and winced at its powerful, bitter notes. Strangely, he quite enjoyed the sharpness of the brew, feeling a hit of caffeine close to that of a double espresso.

"That was one hell of a ride today," Ali said with a grin. "Did you see the size of that snake I nearly hit? Must have been ten feet long."

Five maximum, Hector thought, doing a rough estimate of the road's width in his head. The creature had been lying stretched out in the midday sun, soaking up the heat, when the pair of speeding bikes put the fear of God into it. "Yeah, it was pretty big. I got some incredible shots just after too."

Hector fished out his battered but ever-faithful Canon DSLR from its carry case and flicked it on. He circled the dial on the body, winding at speed through more than a hundred photos, all taken this morning. Rows of monolithic limestone peaks filled many of the frames. Others were taken up by emerald-green paddies, filled with thousands of sweet-scented young rice shoots that had rolled like waves in the ebb and flow of the warm summer breeze.

"This is gonna be one hell of an article," Hector said, feeling pleased that he forced himself to go through with the trip.

"Told you it'd be worth it."

"Yeah, good shout, mate." In the past few weeks, Hector had frequently doubted the value of dropping half his savings to come and visit his friend in Vietnam. But now, with the quality of the images on his camera and the quantity of amusing anecdotes he'd amassed in his notebook, Hector was sure he could earn it back twice over.

"Not exactly your usual style though, eh? No trendy beach bars or Instagram check-in spots up here."

"True. It's definitely grittier than my normal travel stuff. I might do two articles: one commercial, one for fun."

"That's bullshit, man." Ali gave him a cocky grin. "You just gotta believe in yourself a bit. Write what you like and pitch it as is. If any of the big magazines don't bite, then publish it online."

Unlike print articles, Hector's website didn't bring in much income, but it was his place to write about what really interested him. The most frequently viewed posts covered a supposedly haunted abbey in Sussex, a slave plantation in Arkansas, and a Nazi officer's suicide bunker in Poland.

Writing and pitching vanilla topics, however, put a barrier between Hector and potential scathing rejections. It was much easier to handle someone hating his writing if he didn't care that much about it himself.

"Nah. I'd rather sell out." He laughed, trying to sound convincing.

Ricky popped his head through the rear door that led to the garden. His face was dripping with sweat, and the entire front of his gold and black fake Versace T-shirt and jeans covered in dirt.

"Come on. I'll show you guys to your room," he said. "When you get settled, we can have a beer in the hammocks. Then, you can meet *the others*." He raised his eyebrows and smiled, a weird grin that made his eyes pop even more than usual.

"Who are *they* then?" Ali asked.

"Don't worry," Ricky said. "I gotta feeling that you guys are gonna be pleased."

★ ★ ★

Ricky was right, well, half-right at least. A battered grey taxi, speckled with patches of mud, pulled up fifty yards from the house. Understandably, the driver was unwilling to venture any further down the pothole-riddled track, no doubt fearing that he would snap an axle.

Hector lay in the hammock closest to the front of the hut, sipping a near-frozen can of 333, the Vietnamese equivalent of Budweiser that was popular among the American GIs in the wartime. Ali was in the next one over, with a low table sporting four empty cans at his side. The pair watched with intrigue as the dented door of the seven-seater slid back and three figures emerged.

The first person from the car was a seventy-something-year-old grandma, with long, sleek silver hair that caught the fading light. She was wearing a pyjama-like blue cotton outfit, adorned with woven yellow flowers that ran down the right-hand side of the fabric. The lady slowly clambered out, carrying a small suitcase and several see-through pink carrier bags containing what looked like a selection of fruits and leafy greens, then began a steady shuffle towards the building.

"Lying douchebag," Ali muttered, obviously expecting more from Ricky's promises.

Just as Hector turned his attention back to the half-full beer balanced on his chest, a second figure emerged. The young woman had bleached blonde hair that was tied back in a loose ponytail, caramel-coloured skin, and big round glasses that made her look nerdy, in a cute way. She wore a yellow summer dress that exposed her shoulders and trailed off just above her knees, offering a glimpse of her thighs that had no right to be as tanned and toned as they were.

A friend followed a few steps behind. She was tall with sharp features and short, black hair that accentuated her high cheekbones. On her left calf was a bright blue tattoo of a butterfly that looked like she had chosen it directly off the shop's wall one night as the result of a few too many drinks. But it was her attire that made her stand out the most. She wore an almost see-through white crop top with a black bra underneath and a pair of tight leather shorts.

Ali's eyes were out on stalks. "Holy shit!" he slurred in a heavy Aussie drawl, his accent thickened by excitement and five cans of lager. He slapped an open palm on Hector's chest with childlike enthusiasm. "This just got interesting. Come on, mate. Let's go over."

The huge Australian sprung from his hammock, spilling his beer in the fervour, and jogged straight over to the group. He shook the two young women's hands and offered to take their bags, giving no thought to the senior citizen as she trudged by on uneven ground and unstable feet.

The old woman reminded Hector a little of his own grandma, the way she hobbled from side to side as she walked, looking like she might teeter over any minute. He pulled himself up, feeling a little lightheaded from the combination of heat and alcohol, and plodded over.

Seeing that Ali already had the younger women's attention, with both of their bags slung over his broad shoulders, Hector walked up to the remaining guest. *Probably better leaving Ali to do his thing anyway.*

"Do you need some help?"

She looked at him for a moment. Her round, wrinkled face crumpled as she frowned in either anger or confusion. Hector wasn't sure which.

He went to reach for her bag but stopped himself, figuring she might think he was trying to rob her. Instead, he offered an arm for her to lean on. A grin spread across the grandma's weathered face and her eyes lit up.

She started chatting with him as they walked. Hector just nodded and smiled, feeling more than a little awkward with the elderly woman who he couldn't even understand, hanging off his arm.

The girl with the blonde hair caught up a second later and exchanged a couple of words with Hector's new friend, then took the bag. She smiled at him. "Hoa says thanks."

"No problem," Hector mumbled. "It looked like you guys were all set anyway."

He glanced over his shoulder at Ali, just a few steps behind, who already had the second girl giggling flirtatiously.

"I'm Bao An, by the way," she said in flawless English. "But you can call me Anna."

"Hector," he replied. "I guess you know Ali already?"

"Yeah, he didn't waste any time making friends." The Australian's booming laugh cut through the quiet calm of the countryside twilight.

"My friend is Hien," Anna said as they walked. "But we call her Em."

Hector turned back to look, and Em gave him a wave.

"We weren't expecting there to be many people staying here," Anna continued. "It's not really a tourist spot." She chuckled, with a geeky, nasal tone.

"Yeah, I can tell," Hector said. "It's hardly teeming with activity out this way."

She furrowed her brow in mock offence.

"We're just here for a night or two," he continued. "Me and Ali are driving north to south. I'm a travel writer."

"Really?"

"Yeah, I'm working on an article about your country for a magazine."

"Oh, that's great! You sound like a very interesting guy."

Hector shrugged, pleased but unsure how to take the compliment. "What about you two? Do you live around here?"

She laughed. "No. Fortunately not."

"Oh, okay. Are you on holiday or something then?"

Anna lowered her voice. "It's a long story." She nodded to the beer cans below the hammock as they reached the hut. "Maybe I'll tell you over a drink later."

Hector smiled. Things were going unusually well. He really hoped he wasn't going to fuck it up like usual. "Sounds like a plan."

Chapter Three

Day Zero
18:55
Present Day

Beneath the raised first-floor of the hut, the stage was being set for a court of mismatched travellers to convene. The sun had since fallen away. Chirping cicadas filled the trees, and the barks of toads in nearby ponds echoed through the night sky.

Hector helped Ricky untie the two hammocks at the front and stow them away in a storeroom behind the hut. On Van's orders, the three men then brought out a long wooden table and seven chairs, each made of lightweight rattan strips bound with bamboo twine. Even halfway across the world, in an unfamiliar culture, Hector found the situation strangely reminiscent of being back at home with his family.

While they set up, Ricky explained that it was a custom for the men to sit on one side of the table and the women on the other. This did not include his mother, however, who got to sit at the top and oversee all proceedings as the head of the household. Hector decided not to inquire about Ricky's father.

The reason for the division soon became clear as Ricky lined up bowls, chopsticks, and glasses on both sides. Then, placed shot glasses and individual clay jugs of liquor on the men's side only.

The scent of fat sizzling over charcoal wafted in from the rear of the house where Van was cooking. It made Hector's stomach growl and his mouth water. The heat had been doing a job of quelling his appetite until this point.

Ricky beckoned at him to take a seat, and Hector slid in with Ali on his right. His friend was tapping a pair of chopsticks impatiently on one of the small porcelain bowls as though playing the drums. "Don't do that in front of Mum or the old lady," Ricky said to Ali. "They'll murder you!"

"Why's that, mate?" He lay the chopsticks down beside his bowl.

"Superstition. Meant to summon evil spirits or something. Just tradition nowadays, though, seen as bad manners."

"Gotcha."

Ricky went off to help his mother bring the food through, and a minute later, the old woman joined them. She was now adorned in a slightly different coloured, yet almost identical, set of cotton robes. She bustled around the table for a moment, rearranging bowls and chopsticks, tutting as she went before, thankfully, deciding on her place close to the top where Van would be sitting.

Casually pushing through a haze of moths and mosquitoes in front of the house, Ricky strolled over. He was carrying a large wicker tray with a big white bowl of rice and several plates of steaming bright green sauteed vegetables. Hector could practically taste the salt and garlic on his lips as their host set them down one by one.

At his side, Ali had his eyes closed in some kind of meditative state, trying not to let his hunger get the best of him when he had a pair of beautiful young women to impress imminently.

"I think you met Hoa already, right?" Ricky said, nodding towards the old lady as he finished shifting everything off the tray and started back to the kitchen. "She's got an interesting story. I'll help translate in a bit."

Hoa, Hector, and Ali all awkwardly nodded at each other and muttered random pleasantries in separate languages that neither of the other could understand. After a few seconds of awkward silence, Ali set about trying to teach her the words for different items on the table in English for some unknown reason, while Hoa nodded along and imitated the sounds so alien to her tongue.

Just as she was getting close to producing something that sounded vaguely like the English word for beer, the two young women made their way across from the house proper.

They both had wet hair and as they got closer, carried the smell of flowery shampoo with them. Anna was now wearing a pair of denim knee-length shorts and a white T-shirt with a manga-style cartoon cat on it, blissfully unconcerned about trying to look fashionable, the polar opposite of her friend.

The dark-haired girl wore a sleek, black, silk dress that hung low, showing most of her back and a fair bit of her front. She'd plastered her face with white foundation and bright red lipstick, making her look somewhat like the ghost of Michael Jackson. Hector offered a smile to them, and Anna sat down across from him.

"Hi," she said.

"Ladies, you both look ravishing," Ali answered in his best mock British accent, although the joke seemed lost in translation.

Before either of the women could reply, Ricky returned, muttering at the dog that was hot on his heels, hoping for scraps of meat.

As Ricky set down the second tray of food, Hector examined the plates, at a loss about what kind of animal the fat, square chunks of dark meat must have come from.

"It's wild boar," Anna said, reading the look on his face. "It's a speciality in the highlands, like pork, only more, erm, brawny."

"Brawny?" Hector asked.

"Yes," she answered, feigning annoyance with a smile curling on her thin lips. "That's the word, isn't it?"

"I guess so, *technically*."

"Then you shouldn't mock me! It's really embarrassing when I'm already trying my best."

"Really? Sorry…"

"I'm joking." She rolled her eyes and laughed, snorting slightly. "Had you going, though, technically."

Hector shook his head, smiling. She seemed like the perfect woman, if she wasn't so clearly out of his league. A minute later, Van joined the group, taking her place at the head of the table. She nodded politely to Hoa, then glanced distastefully at Ali and Em, probably resentful that she was no longer the object of the young man's interest.

Van passed one of the clay jugs to Ricky, who poured out four shot glasses of honey-coloured liquid and handed one to each of the men and his mother. She then ordered him to prepare another two for Anna and Em, almost as a challenge. He ran off and returned shortly with another two glasses.

"Cheers," Van said in English, raising the drink. Everyone clinked them together, following her lead, and knocked the liquor back. It was sweet but still had a kick to it. Rather than finish in one, Anna took a sip, then placed the glass down softly beside her bowl.

"I don't like this stuff," she said, noticing Hector looking at her shot.

"But it's so delicious."

"Brings back too many bad memories," she said. "Besides, I can't drink much or else I'll end up like him." She nodded at Ricky, whose face was already glowing bright red despite his tanned skin.

"It's lack of an enzyme that does that," Hector said, hoping to impress her with his obscure scientific knowledge. "It's common in Asia. Basically, means you can't process alcohol properly, like an allergy."

"Hmm."

Hector could tell he was losing her. "Looks like your friend doesn't suffer from the same affliction." Em was already filling up her and Ali's glasses, holding his eye contact the whole time. Hector was *not* looking forward to a long night of hearing them attempt to fuck quietly in the shared dormitory-style room above.

"Tell me about this article you're writing then," Anna said, passing a chunk of the boar from the shared plate in the centre of the table into Hector's bowl, then taking one for herself.

"Sure. I write mostly travel stuff, so when Ali suggested I visit him and we motorbike from north to south on the Ho Chi Minh Trail, I figured it would make a great story. So far, it's been amazing. Vietnam's a stunning country. A little rough round the edges, but that's part of the charm."

"Thanks," Anna said, seeming to take it as a personal compliment. She pushed her round glasses up onto her head, demonstrating that they were probably more for show than functional. "So, will I have seen any of your writing anywhere?"

"Maybe. I've been published in a few places."

"Ah, come on, mate," Ali practically shouted. "He's being modest as fuck. *New York Times*, *The Guardian*, *National Geographic*... this dude's the real deal."

"Thanks." Hector appreciated his friend's attempt to talk him up but could feel his face reddening. "Ali's a writer too. A poet."

"You are?" Em gushed.

"Yeah. My stuff's a bit too intense for the mainstream though, so you probably won't have seen it around."

Sounds about right, Hector thought. In his opinion, Ali was a legitimately great writer, although most of his poetry was both extremely sexual and intensely graphic.

"That's amazing. I'm an artist as well," Em said. "I'll show you." She pulled out her phone and clicked through a few pictures, which Ali seemed to appreciate.

"What about you, Anna?"

"I'm an editor," she replied. "For a fashion and lifestyle magazine. Although, I'm more focused on the writing than the content, as you can probably tell."

Hector glanced down at his own attire and cringed. He was wearing a pair of tattered jeans and an old, checked shirt, stained with splatters of sunscreen and chilli sauce. "To be honest, I don't know the first thing about fashion. But I like your outfit. It doesn't look like you're trying too hard."

Anna chuckled, following his line of sight to her friend. "That's how me and Em know each other," she said, speaking in a hushed tone. "She's a model."

"Really?!" Hector said way too loudly. He quickly wiped the grimace off his face before anyone could see it. He was always surprised how bony and weird-looking most models were. "This doesn't seem like a very stylish place to be hanging out," he continued. "I think I saw someone literally selling second-hand underwear by the side of the road in the last town we passed through."

Anna smirked and Van cleared her throat, obviously catching wind of the remark.

"It's Em's uncle's hometown too," Anna said. "She comes once a year to pray for him on the anniversary of his death. She asked me to come for company. I had some free time so figured, why not?"

Van passed around the rice dish, which they each used to fill up their own small bowls, then signalled for them all to eat. Meanwhile, Ricky refilled everyone's glasses with honey liquor. When he noticed Ali studying the floating bits of half-fermented bees in it, he proudly explained how he killed the hive and pickled it himself.

They all clinked their glasses again and swallowed another shot.

Still a little daunted by the conversation with the beautiful girl, but feeling eased by the buzz of alcohol, Hector picked at another chunk of meat.

"This is delicious," he said to Van.

"Thank you," she replied. "It's very fresh. Ricky just trapped it this morning."

Hector mumbled a congratulatory response, a little unsure why eating the freshly killed wild animal made him feel more guilty than eating one that had come from a supermarket.

"What about Hoa?" he asked, turning back to Anna. "Is she an aunt or something? Ricky said she was interesting."

"No. We don't know her, actually. We just got bundled in the same taxi from the town." She turned to the older woman who was engaged in a conversation with Van and waited for a natural break before enquiring as to her purpose at the tiny guesthouse in the middle of nowhere.

Anna, Ricky, and Van all nodded along with raised eyebrows and gasps, while Hoa told them what seemed to be an intriguing tale.

Ali and Em continued to chat and laugh at the far end of the table while Hector ate quickly, hoping his feeble attempts at using chopsticks would go unnoticed as he basically shovelled food into his mouth from the bowl.

When Hoa finally finished talking, Anna turned back. "Sorry for the long wait," she said, taking a chunk of meat and chewing it with her hand over her mouth. "She certainly does have an exciting story."

"Oh yeah?"

"So, she grew up in a village nearby. Her older brother was a commander during the wartime. He served on an island that's on a lake a couple of miles from here. Apparently, they had an enormous cave that was used like a secret hideout for weapons and people as they ventured along the trail to bring reinforcements to the fighters in the south."

"So, she's come back to see it or something? Where's the brother?"

"That's the point," Ricky said. "There was a battle for the outpost, no survivors... So, she's come to find his bones and take him home."

"She's going to dig him up? You're kidding? How?"

"They have directions, from a... err," Ricky thought for a moment, "a fortune teller—"

"A shaman," Anna cut in.

"Holy crap. Does it work?"

"Hoa seems pretty confident," Anna said. "Apparently, he's helped a lot of her friends find missing relatives before. There's supposed to be a government program that helps find and bring back the remains of missing soldiers, but it's so under-funded and disorganised that most people turn to these shamans instead."

Van interrupted them, "The sad thing is, wherever you dig around here, you'll probably find bones. Maybe half the time the fortune teller is right, the other half... who knows? Most people don't go to the island anymore, though."

"Why not?"

"No one lives there, for a start," Ricky said. "But it's also a sad place, with a sad story. The American soldiers, who were fighting alongside the south, slaughtered all the people at the outpost. Men, women and children, everyone."

"Wow, that's intense." Hector's mind was going a mile a minute. "I'd love to see it!"

Van's tattooed maroon eyebrows nearly reached her hairline. She muttered something under her breath that sounded like it could have been a swear word. "No you wouldn't," she said. "There's a reason why we don't go there."

"Mum, plenty of people still go there," Ricky said. "Besides, are you gonna be the one to tell Hoa she can't go and find her brother's body?"

She followed her son's gaze over to the older woman, who was smiling happily. Without a word of English, she was completely oblivious to the debate going on around her.

Van looked away, deferring the decision to Hoa, and threw back her shot. "Don't do anything stupid," she said to her son. "If the stories are anything to go by, it's more than just a jungle out there."

Chapter Four

Day Zero
19:14
Fifty Years Ago

"Done," Le Bao Sang called, her voice echoing throughout the cavernous space. She admired her work like an expert calligrapher would, examining each brushstroke. She'd field stripped, cleaned, rebuilt, and reloaded the entire Kalashnikov in under six minutes.

"Good," Captain Chien replied. "But you forgot something." Awkwardly reaching across the rough wooden table with his left hand, the disabled ex-officer lifted Sang's weapon and pressed a button near the grip that clunked in response. "If you don't lock the dust cover in place, it could fly off and hit you in the face in the middle of a fight. Take it apart and start again."

"Yes, sir." A year ago, the hard-headed young woman would have fought the order. It had taken her a long time to wrap her head around the fact that all the wealth and social status in the world meant nothing to her brothers and sisters in arms.

Captain Chien hobbled off in the direction of the barracks. Even though he was technically no longer an officer, the old man had been one of the first soldiers stationed at the outpost. After so long, he was treated like a grandfather to those posted on Hill Two Fourteen, who referred to him reverently as 'Captain'.

According to Truong, Sang's husband—although she still felt strange calling him that—Chien had been offered a position in the capital after his injury. The old soldier, however, had spent half his life at war in the jungle and mountains. For him, sitting for the rest of his days behind a desk in the city would have been a fate worse than death. Not for Sang. The final few weeks of their post couldn't go fast enough.

With a sigh, she pulled off the dust cover and released the recoil springs and the bolt carrier. She caught a glimpse of the thick calluses on her hands as she worked, trying to remember when they'd stopped hurting.

"That's a better way to do it, right?" she said, laying everything out in the order it would be reassembled on the table and turned to the man who sat at the far end. Huy just stared off into the darkness. But that wasn't much of a surprise. He hadn't spoken a word to anyone since she arrived nearly a year ago.

"How does this bit clip in?" Khai inquired from her right, struggling to fit the bolt carrier back into his own weapon. The spindly orphan was only twelve, but already seemed more of a soldier than she could ever be.

"Make sure the bolt is in properly and it's sitting flush against the tracks... here." She guided Khai's hand. "See, Huy?" The mute turned and locked eyes with Sang, showing he was listening. "It's polite to answer when someone asks you a question."

Even if everyone else had given up on speaking to the shell-shocked veteran, she was certain that the remnants of a man were still inside there somewhere. All she needed was for him to utter a single word in the next two weeks, and it would prove that she had made some worthwhile contribution to military life on Hill Two Fourteen, no matter how small.

Five minutes later, Sang squeezed the trigger a few times, hearing a satisfying clunk as the ammo-less bolt of the rifle engaged. Captain Chien always said that the young woman's weapon must be her best friend, and that if she took care of her rifle, it would take care of her.

Sang had called her gun "Ares" hoping that giving it a name would help her care for it, as Chien told her she must. She loved Greek myths, where even the gods made errors and suffered the same tragic fates as men. They were so much more realistic that way. Besides, who better to name her rifle after than the deity of war himself? A hated figure with a dangerous and explosive temperament. So far, however, her and Ares's relationship seemed to be pretty one-sided. She cleaned and cared for him every day, while other than firing off the occasional practice shot, he mostly hung around doing nothing.

"Thanks for your help, Huy," she said semi-sarcastically. He looked almost like he was going to reply. Sang rose to her feet and carefully placed Ares back into the steel rack that sat on the northern wall of the cavern. She then stepped carefully over the slick, uneven ground towards the cookfire in the eastern side of the cavern where Grandma Lan was tending a huge, strategically placed aluminium pot.

A straight plume of smoke and steam intertwined, floating upwards. Sang tracked it to the hundred-foot-high ceiling of the vast cavern, where a breeze quickly dispersed the fumes through hundreds of tiny gaps, cracks, and passages.

Despite the many hardships of life beneath the mountain, Sang felt a measure of pride at the resourcefulness of her people. They could cook and stay warm by the fire all day long, yet there would be no trail of smoke for the B-52s to aim for, no sign from above that their stone fortress even existed.

"*Xin Chao Ba,*" Sang said as she approached.

"You're late," the old woman scolded in her mother tongue without even looking up. She then handed Sang a material bag containing half a dozen mud-covered taro vegetables. "These need to be washed."

Without a word of complaint, Sang made her way over to the makeshift barracks. Beside the bamboo and sheet metal structure was a barrel used to collect the rainwater that dripped in through the cracks in the ceiling.

Sang reached inside to find a rusty tin bucket that rattled around at the bottom, but not a trace of liquid. This wasn't surprising, considering that it had been unseasonably dry, not raining for almost two days. *Better go for a climb then.*

Sang paced through the shadows at the rear of the great cave, following one of several steep, narrow pathways that sloped down to a lower level. Fortunately, the rough fractal-like stone that had all once been part of some vast coral reef, provided her with a decent grip.

A string of generator-powered mining lamps ran alongside the western side of the cave and into the main tunnel, some fifty feet to her right. Unfortunately, fuel was scarce these days, so she had to make do with the distant flames and the odd slither of sunlight that crept in through cracks above.

Ahead of the western wall, Sang reached a ten-foot-wide section of flat ground that dropped off into a massive underground river.

She slung the material bag over her shoulder, sunk her weight low and edged carefully towards the lip, until she found the top of the rope ladder.

The tread material was damp and sticky with moss. It swayed under the weight of each step, making her descent to the bottom of the abyss somewhat treacherous.

The height alone didn't faze Sang much. As a young girl, she had often sneaked out from her and her brother's balcony and scaled the trellises up onto the roof of the villa to watch the sun setting over the Red River. Some days, she would challenge herself to walk right to the edge, feeling the thrill of her heart beating and her blood pumping. It was addictive.

The power of the rushing waters below didn't scare her either. The absolute darkness, however, was a different matter. Far below any traces of flickering firelight, the river flowed into a tunnel blacker than any night she had known. Sang shuddered, staring into its hypnotic depths for a few seconds, then broke away and continued her descent.

Sang found her footing on the narrow tin sampan tied to the bottom of the ladder. It clattered against the stone wall in the current, fighting its bindings. When the young woman felt stable, she leaned forward and washed the potato-like vegetables one by one in the icy water.

As she worked, Sang thought back to all she had sacrificed to be here with the man she loved. *A warm bed, good food, daylight…*

It was almost comical how far from the luxurious life of her youth she had come. But this was war. No one had it easy. Now, she and Truong had paid their dues, and there was light at the end of the tunnel, metaphorically, at least.

Sang finished up, hung the sack back over her shoulder, and started to climb. With each rung, she reminded herself… *Thirteen more days.*

Chapter Five

Day Zero
19:34
Present Day

"Come on, it sounds amazing!"

Ali looked far from convinced as he swung side to side in the remaining hammock near the back of the hut. "Mate, we've got less than a week to cover nearly half the country, and I *need* to get a few days on the beach. I haven't surfed for nearly six months. You could get locked up for that shit where I come from!"

"It'll be fine, I promise," Hector said. "We'll just add on an extra day here, and then we can make the time up on the road."

"Nah, fuck that, man. I don't wanna follow some old bird around the forest, digging up other old dead people."

Hector ran a hand through his hair. Despite his relaxed demeanour, Ali could be infuriatingly stubborn when the mood gripped him. "Surely, you can see how interesting this story is, though? You *really* don't want to check out a haunted jungle?"

"Nope. Especially when I got plenty of 'bush' to get into here." Ali raised his eyebrows with a dirty grin and gave a subtle nod over to Em. She was sitting on the bench where they'd had dinner an hour earlier, her feet up on the table, taking a selfie that looked almost directly down the front of her dress. Anna sat opposite, playing on her phone.

"Wait a minute!" Hector said, a smile working its way across his face. "Don't move an inch. Here." He grabbed another beer from a cardboard crate up against one of the beams and chucked it onto his dumbfounded friend's lap. Ali looked suspicious, then shrugged and cracked the 333 open anyway.

Five seconds later, Hector slipped into the seat next to Anna. "Hey. So, I was going to ask Ricky if we could come with them in the morning. I want to write an article about Hoa hunting for her brother's bones—it's really cool."

"Yeah, it's a unique part of the local culture. One of the really interesting things about this region is that there are so many little hidden cultural quirks like this becau—"

"Sorry," he said, cutting her off. "I just have to figure this out quick because I've got a bit of a problem."

"Oh, okay." Anna seemed like she was probably used to getting cut off. He figured freethinkers probably weren't common among the Asian fashion industry crowd. "What's that?"

"Well, Ali was worried about not being able to understand what was going on, and wanted me to ask if you girls would come with us, like guides?"

"He said that?"

"Yep, it's true."

She glanced over at Ali, seeing him slurp his beer while balancing it on his chest, without using his hands.

Anna smirked. "You're a terrible liar."

"I'm really that see-through?" He'd thought it sounded pretty convincing.

She nodded. "Look, I think you guys seem fun, but we're only here for a few of days. It's probably not a good idea."

"Em, what do you think?" Hector said.

She looked up, taking a break from pouting for the camera. "Ali's definitely going?"

"Definitely," Hector replied. "It'll be great. We'll bring some tents, have a barbecue, bring a bottle of wine. Plus, I bet there are some awesome places for photos—waterfalls and stuff. I could do some professional shots for you two." He pointed at the camera bag still sitting on his chair.

"Go on Anna, let's do it. We've got nothing better to do than sit around here anyway."

Anna still looked uncertain, forcing Hector to double down on his own feigned confidence and offer her a convincing smile. "I suppose we could come?"

"It's a deal." Hector quickly stuck out a hand. Before she had a chance to reconsider, he clasped her soft palm and pumped it up and down. "I'll tell Ali you're in. He'll be excited."

Once Hector explained about the girls, tents and wine, Ali came around to the idea pretty soon.

The next step was convincing Ricky. Hector soon found him outside the back door of the house, where he and his mum were squatting beside a big plastic tub filled with dish soap and bowls.

"Sorry," the young man replied after hearing Hector's plan. "According to Hoa and her shaman, Wednesday is the best day to go. It's all about luck and superstition with her generation."

Hector's heart sank. *No*, he decided. *This is too good a story to pass up.*

"Today's Monday, right? Can't you ask her to bring it forward just a day?"

"Nope. I already arranged the boat to take us to the island on Wednesday, then pick us up the next morning."

"Well, how far is it? Couldn't we swim or something?"

"About a mile. But even if we could, you wouldn't want to."

"Why not? A mile is nothing." Hector had been on the swimming team throughout high school and university. He even won a few trophies before growing too lazy to keep up with the rigorous training schedule that was demanded.

Ricky counted the reasons off on his soapy fingers. "Too deep, too many crocs and snakes, too strong current."

"Current? Isn't it in a lake?"

"Yes, but water goes in and comes out fast."

"Shit." Hector thought for a moment. "What if I pay for another boat? How much does it cost?"

"Like a hundred bucks."

"I'll pay it. That way, Hoa can have an extra day of searching if she needs it. *Plus*, you get to keep the money she paid for the boat. Everyone wins."

A spark of excitement glimmered in Ricky's eyes. Hector knew he had his fish on the hook. "I suppose the driver might be busy on Wednesday." The guide grinned his toothy grin. "Maybe we'll have to change our plans."

Hector glanced over at Van, who was scowling as she silently stacked clean bowls beside the tub. The look she shot back to her son was nothing short of murderous.

Ricky laughed, ignoring his mother completely.

This is going to be amazing, Hector thought.

★ ★ ★

On the hard floor of the hut, with only a wicker mat and a thin fold-up mattress between him and the wood, Hector tried to sleep. Unfortunately, tonight was one of those nights when he found his mind wouldn't switch off, even though his body was exhausted from the long drive in the sun.

Things could have been a lot worse though. Fortunately, sharing the room with the old lady, coupled with the fact that Ali had drunk enough booze to take down a fully grown African elephant, meant he had gone straight to sleep rather than trying his luck with Em. This was quite the blessing. As for some unknown reason, Ali was virtually irresistible to any woman who garnered his attention.

To Hector's left, his friend was now snoring like an elephant too, albeit one with an acute sinus infection. The two girls were on the mattresses to his right, Anna closest, then Em next to her. Finally, there was Hoa, who muttered and mumbled softly in her sleep.

Hector amused himself for a while, wondering what it would be like to climb under the covers with Anna. But he could tell already that she wasn't exactly the overtly sexual type. For some reason, this made her even more appealing. Showing a bit of restraint, in his opinion, was a solid indicator of class.

He leaned over and picked up Ali's phone, which was lying at his side. Having only a ten-dollar Nokia that he'd picked up upon entering the country, Hector had been using his friend's phone for the last few days to check emails and catch up on messages.

Today he had a few requests for submissions from obscure publications around the world. Alongside these, there were emails with updates about questions and comments on his website. He tried hard to reply to each of them, no matter how banal or inane. They'd have to wait a week or two this time, but it would be worth it.

Finding nothing pressing to respond to, Hector started to look for information about the island they were planning to visit. He tried a combination of nearby town names and different military-type keywords until he eventually came up with something promising. It appeared to be a mission report from an open-source site of declassified US documents. Hector tapped to open the scan of a file.

Declassified Document - USMC

DATE: ███████████
TO: ███████████
FROM: ███████████

1. This report is submitted by Capt Hank. S. Williams regarding the outcomes of Operation Outcry that occurred on the dates of July 1st-3rd ██████.

2. **Squad details:**
   Sgt Stanley Rickard (Squad Leader/Grenadier) - **MIA**
   Cpl William Truman (Automatic Rifleman) - **KIA**
   PFC Ian Higgs (Rifleman/Scout) — **MIA**
   Amn Michael Watts (on loan from USAF Linguistics Dept')
   (Rifleman/Interpreter) - **MIA**

3. Operation Outcry was launched from Binh Thanh station on 14th ██████. Fireteam Alpha-Four-Nine touched down at approximately ██████ degrees north at 23.14.

   The fireteam was led by Sgt Rickard, an experienced squad leader and one of the most decorated Special Operatives stationed in Central Vietnam. Rickard was chosen specifically for his experience in leading operations in the region and his combat skills, having been captured by the North Vietnamese three years previously and single-handedly dispatching the entire twelve-man squad.

   Rickard's team proceeded with the operation, venturing by an unpowered nautical vehicle to ██████ island.

   Primary orders were to perform reconnaissance on the outpost known locally as Hill Two Fourteen, situated at ██████ degrees latitude and ██████ degrees longitude. Reconnaissance reports were required to include levels of strategic importance, the number of soldiers stationed, and the value of supplies held within the cave system.

   Secondary orders were to sabotage the outpost if possible and cut off one of the major supply routes from the Ho Chi Minh Trail to the insurgency throughout Southern Vietnam, Southern Laos, and Western Cambodia.

Upon interrogation, captured North Vietnam Army (NVA) soldiers refused to provide details about the outpost, but indicated that reinforcements were light, there were no civilians presence on the island, and that the strategic value of the outpost was high. Prisoners were subsequently disposed of.

The last radio transmission came at 17:25 on July 2nd, Sgt Rickard informed his superior, ███████████ about the death of Cpl Truman, who received bullet wounds to the chest from an unknown NVA fighter. This had taken place during an attempt to free a prisoner who was under interrogation.

It was stated by Rickard that he overcame and dispatched the attacker in close-range combat while his squad tended to Cpl Truman's wounds.

Upon last contact with the fireteam, Sgt Rickard outlined his plan of action for July 2nd, when he and the two remaining members of the fireteam intended to assault the outpost shortly after nightfall.

There was no further contact from the members of Operation Outcry, and all were presumed as missing in action, with the exception of Cpl Truman.

Watts's next of kin and commanding officers at the USAF Department of Surveillance and Linguistics were informed of his status. For his role in Operation Outcry, despite a lack of field experience, Watts was awarded the Medal of Honour (2nd Class).

Rickard, for his steadfast dedication to his mission and fearlessness in the face of attacking an enemy stronghold, was awarded the Medal of Honour (1st Class).

Cpl Truman and PFC Higgs were both awarded the medal of honour (3rd class), and their families were granted full payouts of military pensions in their stead.

NOTES: Operation Outcry was considered a success in that for weeks following its execution, air patrols shown no significant activity taking place on Hill Two Fourteen, and the supply route and subsequent supplies were considered to have been disrupted and destroyed.

Hector mulled over what he'd read for a good ten minutes. The official report sounded almost like a movie plot, with a squad of plucky young soldiers going to sabotage an enemy stronghold, more than the one-sided slaughter Hoa and Van had painted the battle to be. The report even noted that there weren't any civilians on the island. *I guess right and wrong are all just a matter of perspective*, he eventually decided.

One thing was for sure though, the sergeant that led the Americans sounded like an absolute badass. Definitely not the kind of person you'd like to run into in a dark alley.

Lying on his side, looking through the gaps in the wooden wall, Hector noticed something moving over by the house. He crept towards the shuttered wooden window and creaked it open an inch to get a better look.

On the stone pathway, beneath the yellow light and swarming insects, Ricky was on his knees, rolling up a tent into a tight cylinder. When he finally finished stuffing it into a case, the tour guide pulled out a head torch, flicked it on and off twice, making sure it worked, and dropped it into a large hiking backpack at his side.

With preparations complete, Ricky gathered up the bags and switched off the outside light, dropping the countryside into absolute blackness.

This is going to be mad, Hector thought, uncertain if the feeling growing in the pit of his stomach was excitement or dread.

Chapter Six

Day One
06:52
Present Day

A thick cloud of black diesel smoke spewed out behind the narrow vessel as it glided across murky green waters.

From where he stood, sinking deeper into the waterlogged bank, Hector could count more than fifty tiny islands. Some were no bigger than a car, while others were huge limestone pillars that reached hundreds of feet into the sky.

Thick, green foliage covered the larger islands. Steam rose from the treetops in the early morning light, giving them an otherworldly glow, while eagles circled the peaks. The birds would dive to the lake every so often when a flicker of silver caught their attention and soar back up moments later with a fish flailing in their talons.

It had taken three trips—and the better part of an hour—on the back of Ricky's battered little Honda Wave moped to get the group down to the lakeside, even though it was only two miles from his house.

Hector and Ali had decided that it was safer not to leave out their expensive rental bikes unguarded in the wilderness overnight. Thus, choosing not to drive themselves, the group had been forced to double or triple up with Ricky.

Anna, Em, and Hoa all went on the first trip, huddled together tightly, in typical Vietnamese style, while Ricky crouched down half in the footwell. Apparently, seeing well over the handlebars wasn't actually a requisite to being able to drive effectively.

Ali and Hector went next, both with a backpack slung over each shoulder and a tent in opposite hands to help counterbalance the bike.

Eventually, the spindly boat up ahead cut off its engines and drifted peacefully towards the shore, leaving little ripples in its wake, like a pebble skimming across the water.

The vessel's hull was a patchy, faded mint green. A blue sheet metal shelter covered most of the deck with four rows of wooden benches beneath it. On top of the shelter, a bright red flag with a yellow star at its centre billowed in the wind.

Hanging on to a rudder at the stern stood a single fisherman wearing a sun-bleached green pith helmet and a baggy grey sports T-shirt.

The driver shouted a greeting to Ricky and tossed him a rope where he stood halfway up the bank. Their guide then heaved the boat in until its bow met the jetty, which was nothing more than a row of blue plastic oil drums covered with slats of wood.

"Let's go," Ricky called back, waving the old woman towards the vessel first. Hoa hobbled down the slope, gripping the rope with one hand and hanging onto Anna with the other until the pair of them made it to the relative safety of the jetty. Em followed just behind.

The driver reached over and tugged each of the women up onto the swaying bow of his vessel. It rocked precariously with each foot that landed on the deck, looking as though a powerful gust of wind might be enough to capsize it.

"Guess I'm up next then," Ali said. He slipped his fake Ray-Ban sunglasses up onto his head and sauntered down the grassy top part of the bank. After a single step out onto the mud, the non-existent grip on his flip-flops gave way. Ali landed with his hands behind him and slid down the hill, his shins slamming into the platform at the bottom with an audible thud. His body jerked forward, and the sunglasses on his head shot out into the deep water.

"Motherfucker!" he yelled, quickly turning red as he clambered onto the jetty. His hands and the back of his denim shorts and vest were covered in a thick layer of rust-coloured mud.

"You alright, mate?" Hector stifled a laugh.

"No! I lost my fucking Ray-Bans," he shouted back. "They cost me four quid on Khaosan Road."

Being careful to learn from his friend's mistake, Hector kept his body weight low and inched down, using the rope to steady himself, until he reached the platform safely.

Both he and Ali, who was obviously still embarrassed from the fall, opted to take the driver's hand as they climbed onto the boat. Ricky threw the rope over the side and deftly hopped on board. Their guide then dropped to a squat on the bow while the driver pushed away from the jetty with a barge pole.

After just a few minutes, they were out in the open water. The engine was coughing and sputtering constantly as they picked up speed, sitting low in the lake.

Hoa had made herself comfortable on the back row of benches, and was snacking on a bag of grapes, spitting the seeds out onto the floor in front of her. Hector always tried his best to be open-minded and respectful of other cultures, but that was pretty damn gross.

Anna and Em pushed up against the port side, taking photos with the misty hills and vast lake as a backdrop. Hector whipped his camera out and joined them, snapping at least fifty shots of the scenery as the first rays of warm, golden sun drifted across the water, making it shimmer and gleam.

Soon after, his shutter found the girls as they posed. Anna definitely looked more awkward in front of the camera than Em, who was blowing air kisses and puckering her lips. *Damn*, Anna was gorgeous, though, even if she somehow didn't seem to realise it.

"That could've gone better," Ali muttered, as he returned from leaning over the edge of the boat, washing his hands off.

"Could've gone a lot worse too… At least you didn't cry." Hector slapped him on the back, feeling a little smug.

"I should've done, mate. Look at this." Ali pointed down towards his shins, grazed and bloody from the ankles up to his knees. Hector winced. He didn't mind a bit of gore, but that looked painful as hell. "Probably gonna end up with tetanus from that shit."

"Yeah, it's pretty bad," Hector agreed. "But if you're gonna start panicking about a disease, I reckon gonorrhoea is probably gonna do you more damage."

"Keep your fucking voice down," he hissed, ducking his head and glancing over at the girls, making sure they hadn't heard. "It was chlamydia anyway." Ali smirked, but Hector wasn't so sure he was joking.

As the boat reached its cruising speed, the volume of the engine dropped down to a hum.

Em, having finally noticed Ali's injuries, was fussing over him, attempting to clean his leg sexily with a roll of old toilet paper, while he winced in pain. Anna stood nearby against the side of the boat, looking a little uncomfortable, although whether that was from the blood or her friend's cringy actions, Hector couldn't be sure.

He packed his DSLR back into the compact black carry case, slung it over his shoulder, and climbed on shaky feet over to the bow. He sat on the raised platform beside Ricky. Their guide was staring out over the water with bug-like eyes, looking thoughtful as he basked in the glow of the morning sun.

Hector glanced over the edge. There were a few fish—long tube-like creatures that swam near the surface—then it seemed to drop off into darkness below. "How deep is the lake?"

"Very. In some places, more than a hundred feet."

Hector whistled in awe.

"There are some real monsters down there too." Ricky nodded towards the back of the boat. "This man, Tien, when he was a teenager, caught a four-hundred-pound catfish. Fed his family for a month!"

"Four-hundred pounds? Surely not, that's more than double my weight."

"Man is not the top of the food chain here. It's why we don't swim in the lake, not far from the shore at least."

"Fair enough." The thought of coming face to face with a beast that size was not one to be relished.

"Anyway," the young guide continued, "Tien is going to *Bong Cat* village on the far side of the lake. He'll drop us off on the north end of the island and pick us up on the southernmost tip tomorrow when he heads back."

"Alright, guys," Ali said, plonking himself down on the warm, mint-painted wood of the bow. "What about this island, then? Why were they fighting for it? Looks like we're in the middle of goddamn nowhere."

"That's the point," Ricky replied. "In the wartime, the supply line passed right through here. To walk round the lake meant going through exposed areas where soldiers could be spotted easily from the air. Crossing the water was much faster and better hidden, but difficult to do in one go, especially in bad weather on a rowboat filled with supplies."

"So, they hid out on the island to break up the trip?"

"Exactly. Then, when they discovered a huge cave system, it became a perfect cache for supplies and troops so that they could move north or south fast without having to worry about being seen by the bombers or gunships."

"Gotcha," Ali said. "But why fight for the island and not just bomb the crap out of it?"

"With so many islands, it was hard for the Americans to know when and where to look. They sent squads to investigate and found the caves eventually."

"What happened after they did?"

"What do you think? Everyone died."

"Everyone?" Hector asked. It seemed hard to imagine the scenario that could have led to such a brutal end. "How?"

"Not sure. No one left to say. Maybe bombs, maybe guns. No one even bothered to take back the island after. The Americans ducked out of the war the following year anyway, so the place was just left abandoned, bodies and all."

"Intense shit," Ali said.

Ricky nodded in agreement.

"So," Hector said, "why does Hoa need to find her brother's body after such a long time? Is it like a closure thing for her?"

"Yeah," the guide said. "But more than that. In Asian culture, you have to pray for your family members and give them offerings, like burning incense to show they haven't been forgotten. If you have some relic of them or a grave to visit, it's better, obviously. Especially for soldiers or people who died in the war. It's meant to stop them becoming 'Hungry Ghosts'," he said with his fingers in air quotes.

"What the fuck's a hungry ghost?"

"It's when people die—usually murdered or something terrible like that. Buddhists say they become hungry, unable to rest, wandering, starving, and thirsty forever."

Hector nodded. He had some vague recollection of learning about this from a Chinese guy who lived on his floor at university.

"Sounds right up your street, mate," Ali said with a grin, and turned back to Ricky. "He's well into all these haunted houses and shit."

"Who is?" Em asked, coming and sitting on his lap. Anna followed a few steps behind.

"Old matey here," Ali answered.

"Only as a sceptic," Hector said, hoping not to come across like a ghost hunter conspiracy nut job.

"You guys don't still believe that hungry ghost bollocks though, do you?" Ali asked, squeezing Em's exposed thigh.

"Stories like these are a part of our culture," Anna replied. "Whether you take them figuratively or literally, they've existed for over four thousand years. They're older than Jesus or even Muhammad."

"Being old doesn't exactly mean something is good though, does it?" Ali nodded at Hoa, who was staring at the island, her face gaunt and fearful.

Hector shook his head as if to say, 'I'm staying out of this one'.

"It's all just superstition, I think," Ricky said. "I mean, I feel sorry for the people who died and respect what they did for us, but the rest of it is just children's stories."

"They serve a purpose, though, don't they?" Hector said, unable to hold back any longer. "Most cultures derive their morality from religion and tales like these. They make people feel like they're above animal instincts, but in reality, we're all just a couple of missed meals away from killing each other. Humans are brutal creatures when it comes down to it."

"I disagree," Anna said matter-of-factly. "I believe that deep down, most people are good and morally upright. They don't want to kill and hurt each other, but war and desperation force them to act like fiends. Personally, I follow the Buddhist school of thought that says taking a life is never justified."

Hector shrugged, not wanting to enter into a debate with her.

"Yeah, that's bullshit, though, isn't it?" Ali said. "What about Hitler? You saying you wouldn't have popped him in the head if you had the chance?"

"Mate," Hector cut in, seeing Anna roll her eyes. "I think she's just saying people are too quick to start fighting and killing one another."

"Bah, hippies," he said, smirking. "Anywa—"

BANG.

Hector jumped as a distant explosion reverberated across the waters, rebounding from each of the scattered islands, stretching out the boom in a distorted, alien manner. "What was that?"

As if in response, the outboard motor suddenly backfired—the sound much louder and closer, but to Hector's ears, distinctly less sharp and violent than the first.

"No one knows," Ricky said. "It's part of the mystery of the island. Same thing happens at the same time every couple of days—seven fourteen—like clockwork. There will be a few more tomorrow morning too. It's why a lot of folks don't go to the place, except for the odd hunter or a fisherman looking for new ground. Like Mum always says, they think 'it's more than just a jungle out there.'"

"She's really superstitious, isn't she?" Hector asked.

"Of course." Ricky grinned, nodding at the two young women. "They all are!"

Anna looked like she was about to complain when he cut her off. "Anyway, there's a small shack that one of the less-worried hunters put up on the coast. That's where we'll stay."

"What's all that about?" Ali whispered to Em, now with his arms wrapped around her waist. Hector shot a glance over to Hoa, who had apparently moved on from eating and was now kneeling where she'd been spitting seeds a few minutes before. With her hands clasped together and her eyes tight shut, the old woman was muttering something fast under her breath.

Ricky sighed. "This is gonna be a long couple of days." He glanced at Hector, looking exasperated already. "Your story better be worth it."

"It will be," Hector answered, hoping he was right. It was too late for him to back out now anyway.

Resolving to make the most of the situation, Hector slid his camera out of the bag and sneakily took a couple of photos of Hoa as she bowed, pressing her head on the floor of the boat in veneration. He *did* love tales like this—the photos, the atmosphere, the stories—almost as much as he loved finding out why they enthralled people so.

Ricky sprung down from the bow, breaking Hector's concentration, and grabbed the thick, wet length of rope. "Get up. We're here."

Chapter Seven

Day One
07:52
Fifty Years Ago

They should be back by now. Sang tried to force the worry from her head and, instead, focused on her task, letting the rhythm and repetition of her hands soothe her racing thoughts.

For the next hour, she worked in silence alongside Grandma Lan. Sang balled up mung beans and some remaining scraps of meat into sticky rice, wrapped the parcels inside a banana leaf with four tight folds, and dropped them into the boiling pot. The food would cook for several hours, sealing in all the energy, and ensuring the food stayed fresh as long as possible. Normally, this was about a week or two, even in the damp humidity of the cavern.

The sticky rice cakes also made an ideal meal for whichever poor recruit was assigned the lookout duty that day. Sang could only imagine how boring it must be to spend eighteen hours perched high on the mountainside beneath a camouflaged tarpaulin, watching the surrounding waters and skies for incoming troops.

It had been twelve days since the last group of walkers—squads of supply soldiers who travelled on foot—passed through Hill Two Fourteen. Grandma Lan had interpreted the lack of contact as an ominous sign, claiming it meant that either supplies were running low, or that the B-52s had simply got more efficient at finding their targets. Sang had chosen not to listen. She had to stay positive, now more than ever.

After a while, her thoughts drifted back to Truong. Although it wasn't uncommon for him and his men to make camp in the forest, she couldn't shake the feeling that something was wrong. *No,* she prayed. *Not so close to the end.*

"Sang!" A cheery voice shook her from dark thoughts as Ly came running over, a huge smile spread across her face. "Are you finished with your work? Can you come and play?"

"I'd love to, sweetheart, but I need to help Grandma Lan. Can we play later?"

Besides her husband, Private Nam's four-year-old daughter, Ly, was one of the few small joys Sang had found while living in the cavern. The little girl's happiness was boundless and pure in the way only a child's could be.

"It's okay," Grandma Lan said in her croaky voice, harshened by fifty years of smoking a dozen pipes of powerful shag tobacco per day. "I'll finish up here. Ly's been waiting for you all morning."

"Thank you." Sang bowed her head quickly and walked off before the grouchy older woman could change her mind.

"What have you got for us this morning?" she asked, brushing some of the knots out of Ly's long black hair with her fingers while they walked. The four-year-old had an imagination that could rival the great poets, always creating new stories and games for them to play together.

"In here." Ly led her over towards the bamboo poles covered in sheet metal and tarpaulins that served as their barracks.

"Now close your eyes." She pulled Sang by the hand over to her father's folding camp bed.

Nam had been on lookout duty since Sunday, so Ly had been sleeping cuddled up to her "big sister" for warmth. Sang enjoyed having someone to hold on to at night more than she dared admit. Despite being husband and wife, in name at least, Truong refused to share her bed, not while his men continued to suffer cold and alone. Besides, after more than a year already, Sang could wait twelve more days.

"Okay, now you can open them." On the spare bed, Ly had arranged four small figures that her father had carved to look like a family. Beside them she'd got an old ammo box, with a few pebbles, scraps of paper, and other bits and pieces to make furniture.

She passed one of the small dolls to Sang and explained how that doll was a big sister and her own was the younger sister. They were both living in a cave, and today was the day they would finally go home to meet their mother in the village. Sang played along, not having the heart to say otherwise.

When they'd finished their game, Ly laid her figure down on the bed and looked up at her "sister" with big brown eyes, full of hope and innocence. "When can *we* go home?"

Sang stroked the girl's hair where it spilled down her shoulders like a black waterfall. "Just two more weeks. Then, when the replacement team arrives, we'll all leave together. I promise."

Ly smiled. "We'll go to my village, right?"

Sang sighed. "We've talked about this dear. We can't go back there. We'll go to the north instead."

"Oh."

"Don't worry, you'll love it. When we get there, I can show you where I grew up. I've got lots of beautiful clothes and toys. Would you like that?"

"Yes." Ly grinned giddily. "Can my mummy come too?"

"Sorry," Sang fixed her gaze on the damp stone floor. "I'm sure you'll see her again one day." The lie was selfish, but it was easier to swallow than to tell the truth. No matter how many times Sang heard Nam explain it, the girl just couldn't, or wouldn't, believe her mother was gone.

It made Sang sick with anger to think of Ly being dragged from the burning wreckage of their village. According to Nam, the Southern Vietnamese planes had desolated her hometown and many more nearby without mercy. All he was able to do amid the carnage was flee with his child, leaving her mother's charred remains to feed the crows. *At least she's safe here.*

Chapter Eight

Day One
08:15
Present Day

Hector jumped from the bow of the rocking boat and landed ankle deep in mud. After both he and Ali had found sure footing, they reached back to help Hoa and the girls down, while Ricky and Tien lowered them by the shoulders.

Their guide asked, somehow finding the only dry patch of ground on the steep, wet bank. "Everyone good?" he asked.

"I think so," Hector said, looking first at Hoa, who seemed stable, then over to Anna.

"What's the plan then, chief?" Ali asked, turning to Ricky and shielding his eyes from the blazing sun. "It's hot as a camel's cunt out here."

Both the heat and humidity were already picking up, and the mud underfoot was steaming.

"The hut is about an hour from here, right up on the waterfront. We'll set our tents up there, so we'll have a 'wall' on two sides at least. It should help protect us from any animals that may come wandering through at night. Then, we'll have a rest and go out searching after lunch."

"Wouldn't the waterfront be one of the most dangerous places, though?" Hector said. "Surely, that's where all the predators go to hunt?"

"Dude," Ali cut in. "He's a pro. He knows his shit."

Hector bit his lip and shrugged. "Sorry."

"Lead on, bro."

As Ricky casually strolled up the bank, leading the line of unlikely companions, Hector hung back, taking a few photographs before the group disappeared into the shadows of the trees.

The boat soon chugged away, passing behind another small island, leaving them with only the sound of its sputtering outboard motor echoing across the lake. Just ten footsteps into the jungle, the chorus of nature drowned it out completely.

Tiny, colourful birds squawked and chattered overhead. Somewhere far off, the howl of a monkey rang out, while the buzz of mosquitoes and rustling of lizards among the foliage gave Hector a sense of being somewhere truly wild.

As they tramped through the forest, near enough untouched by humanity for decades, it was clear that Mother Nature had certainly reclaimed this land.

Hector broke into a little jog until he caught up with Ricky, who was leading the procession. Behind him, Anna strolled with her arm linked through Hoa's, supporting the old woman, not that she seemed to need it. At the rear, Ali walked with Em, the two of them laughing and touching each other constantly in a flirty manner.

Em's thick makeup was dripping down her face and running into her low-cut tank top, making her look a bit like a waxwork model melting under a spotlight. Meanwhile, her exposed legs were already dotted with patches of puckered pink flesh from mosquito bites. Hector shook his head. *It's a hundred degrees out here. Doesn't anything ever put him off?* Despite the conditions, his friend's perseverance and dedication to getting laid was strangely inspiring.

"How big is the island?" Hector turned back to Ricky, still panting slightly from his jog to the front. The air was humid, thick with spores and the taste of rotten fruit, which made it hard to catch his breath.

"About four miles round the outside. Maybe one or a little more across, but you can't go over the mountain without some serious equipment. Too steep."

"Oh, that's not as bad as I thought."

"Yes, but it's slow to walk. This is the only man-made path. The rest means picking through trees and following animal trails, which takes a long time."

Hector nodded and fell back to Anna and Hoa.

"Hi." Anna gave him a smile.

"I was wondering, how does Hoa know exactly where to look? Did the shaman give her a map or something?"

Anna translated the question and the old woman replied. "She says he described it all in detail. The site is on the south side of the island, near the caves where the outpost used to be."

"How do they actually do the process?" The thought of it puzzled Hector. Would the shaman have done research on the site? Could it all just be guesswork?

Anna translated again and Hoa went into a lengthy explanation as she trudged onwards, not missing a step. The old woman was obviously tougher than she looked.

"She says you need to bring a photo or a possession from the person you are looking for and pay the shaman with gold. He then burns incense and prays, focusing on the object. This channels a spirit— either her brother or a deity of the dead. Sometimes, many spirits in a row. They take control of the shaman and speak through him in an ancient language while an assistant transcribes it all. Finally, you have to pay someone to translate the script back to modern language."

"Wow. So, it's like necromancy. Is the process expensive?"

Hoa nodded vigorously and explained.

"It cost her hundreds of millions of Vietnamese Dong... thousands of dollars. That's why she only has one chance. She's been saving for a decade, praying she'd be able to find her brother while she was still healthy enough to make the trip."

"That's amazing. Well, tell her from me she's a strong woman. I can't imagine how much this means to her."

Hoa smiled and patted him on the shoulder.

"She says she hopes you'll never have to know."

Hector held Hoa's gaze for a second, feeling a strange connection with the old woman. He too, knew what it was like to lose someone you were close to.

Another half hour of trudging through the near-airless forest passed before they finally reached their destination. Hector grimaced as they emerged into the clearing, although he wasn't actually sure what he'd been expecting.

A mouldy, dilapidated shack nestled up against a thick patch of trees to their left. It faced out towards the water, leaving twenty feet of patchy grass between it and the lake.

Moss-covered wooden panels rose just seven or eight feet high, and the structure was capped with a rusty tin roof.

Ricky led the way towards the hut and tugged on the rough wooden door. After three tries, it eventually swung open, revealing a fifteen-foot-long room intersected with shafts of sunlight that pierced through the holes in the roof. A waft of cool, sour air, carrying the lingering aroma of old charcoal, slapped Hector in the face.

In the centre of the shack was a blackened bundle of logs, where someone had lit a fire on the dirt floor. Around the remnants of the fire, shards of shattered green glass and patches of something brown that could have been blood spotted the earth. Sticking out of the ground on the far side was an eight-inch-long knife. The material that had once wrapped its handle was burnt to a crisp, as if it had been thrown in the flames, then pulled back out.

"What the fuck?" Ricky said, in a high-pitched tone, as he clamped eyes on the bizarre scene.

"Shit, mate." Ali leaned in over his and Hector's shoulders with ease. "Looks like someone got messed right up in here."

"I thought no one lived on the island?" Anna said.

"They don't," Ricky replied. "Maybe a hunter or fisherman got injured and spent the night; they come here from time to time."

Hector whipped out his camera and took a few shots of the scene, the shafts of light falling from above giving it a ghostly look. He crept past Ricky and edged round the spent fire, taking a close-up of the group's multitude of expressions as they peered in. He then picked up the knife, studying its blade.

"USMC," he said, running his fingers over the embossed lettering just above the handle. "Any ideas?"

"U Suck My Cock?" Ali offered, looking around at the grim faces for a laugh, but none came.

"United States Marine Corps," Ricky muttered. "Whoever had the fire must have found it. That would explain why it's burnt. Traditionally, people burn things to send them to the spirits, like incense."

"Bet it's worth a few bucks," Ali said, reaching for the blade.

"No way." Hector slapped his hand away, surprising even himself with how strongly he felt about it. "Have some respect for the people who died here. We're not looting their stuff to sell."

"Oh, come on, mate. Don't tell me you're buying into all this superstition now?"

"It's not superstition," Anna pitched in. "Just not a good idea to take a weapon that's been involved in a brutal war home for novelty or profit. It's disrespectful."

"I agree," Em said.

"Me too." Ricky replied. Anna translated for Hoa, who leapt into a rant at the Australian, wagging her finger in his face and scolding him in a torrent of foreign words.

"Fine," Ali relented. "Leave it then, Jesus. Let's just get set up. I'm starving."

"We should pitch the tents in a circle facing inwards," Ricky said, "and build a fire in the middle to keep away bugs or anything bigger." Their guide dropped his oversized backpack.

Hector's stomach was growling as well. The heat of the walk had made it surprisingly hard going. He'd need a good meal and a lot of water if he hoped to get through the rest of what looked like it was going to be a *very* long day.

Ricky, Anna, and Em worked together to pitch two of the tents, while Hector and Ali got started on the third. Hoa sat on the step of the hut, fanning herself with a purple silk hand fan.

The two foreigners were embarrassingly slow at putting up their tent. It took a good fifteen minutes of profuse sweating and swearing just to plug all the poles into place. By the time they were ready to start clipping the cover and interior together, the other two tents were already standing proudly.

Em disappeared inside one and Hoa into the other. Anna and Ricky then wandered over, muttering and grinning, obviously finding Hector and Ali's progress, or lack thereof, greatly amusing.

"You look like you could use a hand," Anna said with a smile, her long, blonde hair back-lit by the sun reflecting off the water.

"It's okay, we've got it," Hector replied, feeling a blush creep up his cheeks.

Although too nice to disagree, she obviously wasn't fooled and immediately set about unplugging the poles he'd attached in the wrong place.

"I'm not normally so bad at this stuff," he said. "But it's been about a decade since I last tried to pitch a tent."

"Are you sure you're not just afraid that you can't keep up with me?" She gave him a wink.

"How come you guys are all so good at this?"

"Tour guide," Ricky said, as if it was obvious, taking the poles from Ali's hand and snapping them into place quickly.

"What about you and Em?" Hector asked as Anna took his set of poles and bent them into place, raising the interior of the tent. "You guys look so casual and unfazed in the jungle too."

"We all do basic training."

"Training? For what?"

"The army. It's a part of our education. Everyone gets a few months of studying survival in the mountains. Hunting, making camps, how to shoot, stuff like that."

"Damn," Ali chipped in before Hector could respond. "No wonder you guys won the war... Last year, I shot a rocket launcher at an old car on a firing range in Cambodia. That was pretty badass; cost me, like, two hundred bucks, though."

"We definitely don't do that." Anna laughed. "Mainly pistols and rifles, in case we ever need to be called up for service."

"Fuck, I'd love to unload an AK into something. That would be rad!"

"Yeah, it's fun. As long as you never actually have to shoot at someone, of course. I couldn't even imagine how horrific that would be."

"Alright, we're nearly done here guys," Ricky said, fastening the final clip into place. "Now, how about you two guys share this one? I'll go with Hoa, and the two girls can have that one." He pointed to the tent with Em inside.

"I got a better plan than that, chief." Ali winked at his friend.

It didn't take long to figure out the sleeping arrangements. Hector and Ricky would bunk together, while Em persuaded Anna to share with Hoa so she could double up with Ali. None in the group seemed particularly enthralled by the prospect of having to hear the pair fuck all night with nothing but a couple of layers of canvas as soundproofing. However, it didn't seem likely that anyone would be able to stop them.

Ricky gathered a few fallen branches from nearby and took some of the dry bits of half-burnt charcoal from the hut. With a squirt from a bottle of ethanol that he had in his bag and a lighter, a fire was soon burning in the centre of the camp. The guide then produced a small pan and a couple of tins of stewed meat from his backpack, along with some weird-looking tubes of bamboo.

Obviously well accustomed to camping, Ricky fried the meat beautifully and handed out the tubes, showing Hector and Ali how to peel back the outside, revealing a portion of white sticky rice that had been stuffed inside to ferment. It had a naturally sweet, smoky taste to it.

The guide handed out pairs of bamboo chopsticks, and the group took turns dipping their rice in the sauce and fishing bits of meat straight out from the pan.

Not in the habit of taking a siesta like the others, Hector sat down at the entryway to the hut. There he scribbled a few notes in the glittery-pink, unicorn-emblazoned notebook he kept in his camera bag. Unfortunately, it was the only one they had in stock at the village store when he ran out of space in his old notebook a few days before.

Hector jotted down a few details of the boat ride that he didn't want to forget. The depth of the water, the story of the fish Ricky's friend had caught, and their discussion about the dead, which seemed to have become somewhat of a theme on this trip.

So far on travels with Ali, Hector had seen dozens of photograph-adorned shrines in the corners of people's front rooms stacked with incense and gifts to the departed. The local culture seemed to be much more in touch with death than people were in Britain, facing it directly rather than walking on eggshells around the subject. Anna had even explained to him about traditional customs where people would bury their loved ones for a few years, then, later, dig them back up to be cremated. Although to Hector, this seemed a step too far.

After letting his mind wander for a while, Hector's thoughts returned to the current trip and the mysterious sounds that were heard at the same time every two days. That bit, in particular, stirred his imagination. *Maybe it's something geological? Like the Old Faithful geyser, that's pretty reliable with its timing.*

Finally, he started noting the scents and sights of the walk, the morbid surprise of the blood-stained shack, and the USMC knife.

Ali poured a cup of coffee and took a sip of the powerful bitter-smelling brew, nodding his head in approval. He poured a second cup for Hector and came to join his friend on the step.

"This is all going pretty well, isn't it?"

"Absolutely. It's gonna make one hell of a story."

"I was talking about the girls, actually."

"Oh."

Ali grinned. "But either way, you're right, it's gonna be fucking mad if we actually find her brother!"

"Yeah, that would be pretty hard to explain rationally, especially if there is something to identify him—a uniform, or a dog tag or something?"

"I wouldn't get your hopes up, mate."

"Well, even if we don't, then it's still a privilege to come and help Hoa to look and document it." Hector glanced over his shoulder at the blood-splattered hut, then at the thick jungle to its rear. "Also, I reckon this place is gonna be pretty damn creepy at night."

"Good."

"Why good?"

Ali nodded over to the tent, where the outline of Em getting changed was just about visible through the canvas. "You won't be too surprised if you get woken up by screaming."

Hector spat out a mouthful of coffee all over the ground, doing his best to fight laughter as the liquid burnt its way up and out through his nose. "As long as it's not you screaming, then I could live with that."

"I prefer to grunt."

Hector cringed. "You're disgusting."

"You should try it sometime." Ali lowered his voice. "Seriously, though, I reckon the other girl would be game too. Just be confident with her and you'll have it in the bag."

"Shh," he hissed. If Anna was awake, she'd have heard every word. Hector had never particularly struggled with women, but that didn't stop him from worrying that she would laugh in his face if he tried to kiss her.

"I've got a bottle of vodka in the tent," Ali said. "Just have a few drinks tonight to loosen up a little, then make a move on her. What's the worst that could happen?"

"Okay, okay," Hector replied, trying to end the conversation as fast as possible, glancing nervously over towards the tent.

After another twenty minutes, they heard the rustles and zips of bags opening, and people preparing for the afternoon's hike.

"Right, I'm gonna go dig out some sun cream," Ali said. "My neck is already red as the devil's dick."

"Try wearing a shirt sometimes. Or if you *really* can't bear it, then look in my bag. I've got some factor fifty."

"No thanks, mate. That's probably why you're as pasty as a ghost. I got some oil somewhere, factor five, gotta keep my tan solid."

"You'll be doing serious damage to yourself using that stuff. Skin cancer could kill you, you know."

"Bullshit. I'm gonna die in an epic blaze of glory, or I'm straight up not gonna die... like Keith Richards."

Ali laughed and clambered over to the tent, just as it unzipped and Anna emerged.

Sensing preparations were underway, Hoa came out too, and began nervously checking through her bag and cleaning up around the camp.

"Can I have a bit of that coffee, please?" Anna said from the doorway, pointing to the pot steaming near Hector's feet.

"Sure. But you'll have to use one of our cups. Apparently, Ricky only brought two."

"No problem," she said, walking over. Hector quickly slipped the pink notebook from his lap back into the camera bag before she got close enough to see it.

Anna had changed into a pair of sports trousers, a tight, long-sleeved T-shirt and a baseball cap, covering up to keep the sun and bugs away. Hector thought it was a pretty reasonable choice of attire for a jungle exhumation and wondered who would dress the least appropriately out of Ali and Em. Now that he thought about it, they were pretty much perfect for each other.

He poured Anna a cup and passed it over. She blew the steam away and took a sip.

"I heard what you were talking about earlier, by the way."

"Oh. Yeah, sorry," Hector laughed sheepishly.

"Ali's a funny guy, isn't he?"

"Hmm," he said, trying not to agree too strongly. Ali *was* funny, in his own crude childish way.

"Well, just so you know," Anna added, rising to her feet and flashing Hector an alluring smile. "I wouldn't mind too much if you made a move on me. I might not even fight you off."

She walked over to the tents without so much as looking back, leaving him dumbfounded at this confident, sexy side that Anna had kept hidden so far.

"Oh, I forgot to tell you," she said, turning on the spot. "We have to be there at the exact right time, so get ready and don't forget your spade!"

Hector laughed nervously. It hadn't really sunk in before now that he may actually be digging up a human corpse today.

Chapter Nine

May 21ˢᵗ

05:25

Fifty-Three Years Ago

The mosquito that had been buzzing around the hut all night finally settled. Stanley Rickard inched his right arm forward, then exploded like a coiled viper.

With a cupped hand, he snatched the malarial bastard from the soft skin of Linh's back and crushed it, leaving congealed black blood smeared across his palm.

Not her, he thought, recalling the horrific fever, cramps, and vomiting that had made recovering from his injuries so slow. Someone weaker would probably have let themselves succumb to the combination of disease and a gunshot wound, but not him.

Rickard rested his head back down on the hard bamboo mat that had been his "bed" for the better part of three months. That this thing could even be considered a bed seemed criminal. In fact, it was so hard, it almost made him miss the bunks back in Jacksonville, and that was really saying something.

Linh stirred, her long eyelashes flickering, and a sweet smile spreading across her face as she realised that she had fallen asleep in his arms, *again*.

"I have to get back," she murmured, still only half-awake.

Linh took her time dragging herself up to a sitting position and kicked the cover off to reveal her naked figure. Rickard felt a stirring and reached out, running his hand up her thigh. "Why go? They clearly all know anyway."

"You know why!" She smiled, a cute expression that was tinged with guilt, and slapped his hand away. When Rickard played dumb, she explained again. "Because my father is a traditional man and likes to pretend that he doesn't know about us."

The American couldn't help but feel a little guilty himself. Bao, Linh's father, had saved his life; and how had Rickard repaid the kindly old villager? By taking his eldest daughter to bed.

"As long as we keep doing *this*," Linh said with a playful smile, "I want to keep up the illusion."

She laughed, and Rickard laughed with her. Her joy for life was infectious. In fact, that feeling was something, he now realised, had been absent from his life for far too long.

He'd known Linh for less than three months. The first few weeks, Rickard had mostly been bedridden, slipping in and out of consciousness, fighting off a fever due to the combination of an infected wound and a bout of malaria.

Finally, a heavy dose of herbal remedies, an array of mysterious tablets that Bao had acquired from the next town over, and the soldier's own emergency supply of antimalarials had helped him battle through the worst of it.

When he realised Rickard was going to pull through, Bao arranged a more permanent place for him to stay while he recovered. It was a small building that belonged to a neighbour's son who had gone off to fight for the South.

Bao instructed his daughter to check in on Rickard and help change his dressings and clothes. Kind, but foolish, the old man still thought of Linh as a child, despite her being nearly twenty.

One day, while she was helping him put on a shirt—it was difficult with one injured arm—Rickard noticed she was looking hungrily at his bare chest and knew right then that she wanted him as much as he wanted her. Later that night, he'd awoken in the darkness to someone slipping into his bed.

That had been the first of many enjoyable nights. Unfortunately, by now Rickard knew their time together couldn't last much longer. He'd have to return to his people or face desertion charges.

Although he didn't relish the thought of leaving Linh, especially knowing how she'd be treated after he departed.

Everyone in the village knew what was going on between the two of them. He could see it in their sideways glances and slight frowns when he passed, even though they said nothing.

She's young, Rickard told himself. *They'll all forget I even existed in a year or two.* However, he harboured his own doubts. She'd probably never be able to find a husband or get a decent job after their affair. Most likely, she'd grow older and bitter at him for leading her astray. Meanwhile, to him, she would be just a sweet, distant memory—a brief bubble of joy surrounded on all sides by fighting and war.

Rickard wrapped one arm around Linh's stomach as he sat half-upright against the wall. With the other, he reached back for the packet of Lucky Strike cigarettes that was lying alongside his Smith and Wesson at the side of the bed. He always kept both of them close. Rickard flicked the packet open. *Three left. Shit.* It was even worse than he thought.

The American decided he could wait a while longer, and laid back down, closing his eyes. He breathed in Linh's scent, finding comfort in that rather than the smoke. *Maybe I could stay?*

With his eyes closed, Rickard summoned the soldier's discipline inside of him, and banished any foolish sentiment from his head.

Apart from his shoulder throbbing in the damp weather, he was pretty much healed. He needed to leave, and soon, otherwise it would become impossible. *Just a few more days.*

Chapter Ten

Day One
12:22
Present Day

Hector pulled his camera bag over his head and slathered on a second layer of sun cream. By the time he was finished, both Ricky and Em were still yet to emerge.

Instead of hanging around the tents, he wandered over to Hoa and Anna, who were standing chatting on the path before the clearing.

"*Chao*, Hec-tor," Hoa said, giving him a polite nod. She then went back to flicking through a thick, leather-bound book that looked like some kind of handwritten encyclopaedia, pointing out certain parts to Anna.

Hector leaned in to get a better look, figuring it must contain the transcript of the necromancy.

"Could I take some shots of it, please?" he pointed to the text and mimed taking a picture.

Hoa nodded and passed the book over. Hector whipped out his camera, making sure he caught a good angle of the red leather binding, the gold bordered pages inside, and the decorative script that ran side to side in swirling onyx-black ink. Overall, it looked strikingly high quality and professional.

Hector flipped through the sheets of paper, surprised at how much information the book seemed to contain. It was at least two hundred pages long. "What does it all say?"

Hoa caught on and started explaining to Anna. "Most of the text comes from different deities. It talks about her brother; at first, giving some facts to confirm they're in contact with the right person."

"Let me guess," Hector said. "It says some random family members' names, talks about fights with his loved ones, and speaks about a health problem?"

She nodded, not daring to make eye contact with Hoa.

"Classic cold reading," he muttered, suddenly feeling a little guilty as he looked into the old woman's hopeful eyes. "But that takes nothing away from it. If the process helps her get closure, then who cares, right?"

They continued to flick through, taking occasional photos. Then, about halfway, came across one page that was different from the others. A single quote was written in huge black brushstrokes, filling the whole sheet.

"What does this say?"

"Oh," Anna's eyes widened, either in excitement or shock. "This section is actual quotes from her brother when he possessed the shaman. It says something like…" She thought for a moment, trying to figure out the best way to translate the meaning. "The innocent and the evil suffer alike for the sins of war. Release us from our eternal torment."

"Wow, that's pretty heavy stuff."

"Yeah. It's probably why she's so dedicated to finding his body. I can only imagine how bad it must be to think that someone you love is innocent and destined to suffer endlessly."

Hector narrowed his eyes. "Surely, you don't think that means her brother is the innocent one? You can't be free of responsibility if you're a soldier fighting in a war. That's impossible."

Anna scowled at him. "There were a lot of people forced to fight on both sides. Not just professional soldiers, but people who had to enlist simply to survive."

"Okay, sorry." Hector obviously knew a lot less about the situation than he thought. Until now, he'd kind of assumed that the Vietnamese soldiers had all been hard-line Communist patriots rather than actual people just going about their lives.

"Anna, can you help me translate something please?" he said, hoping to change the subject. "I want to ask if Hoa minds me taking photographs while we dig?"

She repeated the question. "It's okay," Anna answered. "But Hoa asks if, when we're done, she could have some copies of your photos to put alongside the altar where she'll keep her brother's remains."

Even though he was more than happy to share any of his images, Hector couldn't help feeling that the old woman was setting herself up for heartbreak.

"Of course," he said, and reached out to shake Hoa's hand. Her palm was cold and wrinkled, but her grip had a surprising, determined strength. It was nearly enough to make him second guess his reservations.

A minute later, Ricky, Ali, and Em made their way over. "Let's get moving," Ricky said. "We've got a schedule to keep."

An hour into the hike, they ventured close to the base of the mountain. The huge, forested peak loomed over them looking far more ominous than it had done from the waterfront.

As the jungle grew thicker, Hector could have sworn he felt eyes on the back of his neck. It was a sensation that he couldn't quite explain, but decided to try to ignore, rather than risk looking paranoid in front of Anna and the others.

With Ricky and Hoa leading the way, they continued at a slower pace, picking through the undergrowth among the trees, and trying their best to follow the "map" that seemed to be made up entirely of cryptic, treasure-hunt style descriptions. *Two hundred paces west. Turn towards the sun...*

Finally, they entered a small grove. The trees seemed to retreat and arch away from the centre, growing sporadically as if a great wind had blown through a patch of crops. Or more likely, some explosion in the past had felled them and they had then regrown around the damaged land.

Ricky paused, double checking his map. A breeze wafted in from above, making the stifling humidity a touch more bearable as Hector, Anna, Em, and Ali stepped up beside him.

The mini clearing was no more than ten feet across. Their guide checked the map again. "This is it," he announced with a smile, looking proud of his handiwork.

Ricky pulled two folding military spades from the side of his huge backpack. Each had a triangular-shaped trough, with one edge serrated for cutting and one that was razor sharp, like an axe. "Who's digging first?" he asked, looking at the two other men.

"Fuck it, I'll go," Ali answered, probably hoping that the sight of him building up a sheen of sweat across his rippling muscles might make Em equally moist.

Ali and Ricky dug a shallow trench along the length of the space, while Hoa stood over them, commenting on their work as though she were the foreman of some kind of bizarre building site.

Hector noted the old woman's arched back and calloused hands. She'd obviously spent a lifetime farming and knew what she wanted to see in a pit. Ricky didn't seem to mind, but Ali grimaced, getting noticeably more and more irritated with each comment.

As they worked, Hector snapped a few shots, then made notes in his sparkly unicorn notebook about the time of day, the thick musky scent of the forest, and the pungent aroma of wood smoke on his clothes.

After twenty minutes, drenched in sweat and covered in a fresh layer of soil, Ali tapped out. Calling his buddy over to take his place, the Australian went to lie in the shade.

"How deep are we going?" Hector asked, following Ricky's lead as he stepped methodically forward with each scoop and heaved the soil out to the right side of the pit.

"Not too far," their guide replied. "Just a couple of feet. Since the outpost was abandoned, the bodies would have got covered naturally by mud, leaves, and whatever other debris the storms carried in."

The work was hard and heavy, but eventually Hector found his rhythm. It was almost Zen-like— trenching out a scoop, throwing it sideways, taking a breath, and stepping forward. An ongoing cycle of movement, sweat, and dirt. They soon hit two feet in depth but found nothing.

Hoa's face had fallen from wide-eyed excitement to sorrow as she stood over the diggers, shivering despite the sun beating down on her shoulders. Anna eventually persuaded the old woman to sit with her in the shade of a nearby tree.

It was a good move. They had nearly the entire afternoon and a full night before their transport back to the mainland arrived. In the meantime, if Hoa, or any of them for that matter, came down with heatstroke, it could be a death sentence.

Hector wiped the sweat from his face with his sleeve and smiled at Anna, who was fanning Hoa and holding a bottle of water on her lap. Meanwhile, Em was lying beside an exhausted Ali, taking selfies while pouting at the camera.

He took another step and thrust the spade into the ground. With a dull clang, the tool vibrated in Hector's hands and a buzz of excitement shot through his veins. *We've only gone and found him!*

Chapter Eleven

Day One
14:12
Fifty Years Ago

Muffled voices shook Sang awake, forcing her to emerge from beneath the scratchy green blanket. Sleeping through the hottest part of the day was a habit that remained from the times before the war. In the cavern, however, it didn't matter how high the sun was overhead. Darkness and cold reigned supreme.

The voices grew louder, bouncing down the narrow stone shaft that led deep into the mountain. Usually, this was a good sign. If it wasn't their own men returning, it would mean walkers—new people to talk to, bringing vital supplies and news carried down from the north. But today, something about the urgency of the words told Sang this was no joyful visit.

She listened out for Truong, hoping to hear her husband's deep commanding tone, but the voices were too far and too distorted by the stone reverberations for her to make anything out with certainty.

Sang slid from the camp bed, being careful not to wake Ly, who had fallen asleep cuddled up to her. This was something the poor girl did often when her father was out on patrol. It made Sang cringe when she compared it to the way she grew up, surrounded by love and privilege. She covered Ly up to her neck with the blanket. The little girl stirred and wriggled, but soon settled back down into a peaceful sleep.

The morning's fire had burnt down to a pile of smouldering coals, and the strings of mining lamps along the western side of the cavern hadn't been turned on yet. With only a measly spattering of daylight falling in from the cracks high above, Sang worked her way over the uneven ground to the tunnel. She had to be careful not to twist an ankle on the deceptive horseshoe-shaped ridges that rose from the floor.

She used the sound of rushing water to gauge her distance from the tunnel that ran parallel to the river. A few seconds later, the entrance emerged from the shadows, a deeper shade of black than its surroundings. To Sang, it looked like some kind of huge caterpillar had worked its way through the stone as if it was an apple, leaving a misshapen tube— roughly the height of a man—behind. From there, she let the echoes of the voices be her guide.

After a few dozen yards of ducking and weaving beneath low-hanging growths of rock, and crawling across the damp ground, Sang stumbled, catching her knee on a pillar of stone. She yelped in pain, and the distant conversation instantly stopped.

"Who's there?" a voice called in her native tongue, just a hundred yards or so ahead. Sang's heart jumped at the sound.

"Your wife," she shouted back, with relief overpowering any sense of concern.

Truong and Long slowly emerged from the shadows. Private Long was a heavyset man who had apparently entered the military less than two years before, but had soon distinguished himself as a fighter, earning a transfer to the isolated outpost.

"Where i—" Sang caught the grim look on the two men's faces and cut her question short, realising that the third man of their team wasn't coming back. "Oh, no."

Without a word, she walked up and wrapped her arms around Truong, pulling her head tight into his shoulder. A mixture of relief, sorrow, and anger brought tears to her eyes. "What happened to Nam?"

"He must have seen movement in the forest and gone to investigate. It looks like the Americans interrogated him first."

"Ground soldiers?" Sang's voice trembled. It was impossible. "But they never come this far north."

"Apparently, they do now," Long said. "It was an advance team, only four men. But, obviously skilled, if they got onto the island unnoticed." He turned to Truong. "Which is why we need to move on them now."

"Enough!" her husband exploded, making Sang nearly jump out of her skin.

Long sighed and started walking back towards the cavern—the shuffle of an exhausted, beaten down man.

"When they killed Nam, they were trying to goad us," Truong explained. "The Americans aren't stupid. They want us to attack them and give our position away. It's the only reason they'd send such a small party so far north."

Sang sighed. "So, what do we do?"

"We wait. With a bit of luck, they'll find nothing and move on."

She could see in his eyes that he didn't believe it himself. "After capturing one of our lookouts who was armed and in uniform? You know as well as I do that'll never happen."

He pushed away, just enough that he could see into her eyes. Sang held his gaze; it was rare they ever had even a moment alone together. She wished it could have happened without one of their brothers-in-arms dying first.

"The relief team will be here before the next full moon. With reinforcements, we could chance an attack. We could push them into opposing lines of fire. But it would be stupid to risk going up against them with just Long and I. Not so close to the end."

"But it's not just Long and you."

"No."

"I've been training for months for exa—"

"NO."

Sang bit her lip. "So, what do you expect us to do then? Sit here, hiding like rats in a rice cupboard, and wait until the cat sniffs us out and tears us apart?"

"No. I expect us to do our duty and guard this damn outpost, as our orders have been for the last two years."

"Even if it means we all die in the process?"

"We won't."

Sang decided to try a different tack. Truong was a good man, but his pride and stubbornness, wanting to do everything alone, would be everyone's downfall. He needed her help. "Let me ask you a question. Would you give the same order if I wasn't here?"

Truong sighed, his shoulders sinking and face conflicted. "No."

A wave of anger hit Sang as she thought about Nam lying dead somewhere among the trees.

"When I left my old life to come here, I vowed to stay with you through hell or high water," she said. "Now's the chance for me to prove my worth. Let me fight by your side. I can support you. It's my place."

Truong held her tight. His warmth washed over her. Sang realised only then that she was freezing cold and shivering, but she didn't know when it had begun.

"Long thinks we should attack too. Otherwise, they might try to get a jump on us. Probably one day soon, under cover of nightfall."

Sang pulled back and looked up at Truong's face. All the usual joy in his eyes was absent. Dark circles hung below them. He looked gaunt and frail, a shadow of the handsome man she fell in love with.

"I know you want to do your part," he continued, "but if we fight, then I'll need you to stay with the others. If Long and I are caught or killed, then you, Captain Chien, and Huy will be the last line of defence."

"Basically, we'd be done for." Sang grimaced. The old one-armed captain could probably still shoot. Whether Huy would be with it enough to fight was a different question altogether. "Okay." Sang nodded. Her anger slowly faded, and in its place, the thoughts of death welled up once again. "What am I going to tell her?"

"Let me." Truong pulled Sang close. "I'll make sure Ly knows her father died a hero. Then, Long and I will resupply and head back out. If we can get to the Americans while they're still on the west side of the island, when they're relaxed and trapped on the low ground, we'll be able to take them by surprise."

Sang leaned up and kissed Truong on the lips. "I love you," she said, getting lost in his warmth for a moment. Unfortunately, the mixture of sympathy, sorrow, and guilt in the back of Sang's mind couldn't be held off for long and it soon dragged her back to the waking hell they were living.

Chapter Twelve

Day One
15:38
Present Day

On their knees, pulling handful by handful of thick damp mud from the ground, Hector and Ricky uncovered the object nestled in the dirt.

A mixture of regret but also relief came over Hector as he brushed away the soil around the shape to reveal a rectangular metal box, a foot wide and two-thirds of that long. It had to be better than unearthing the bundle of decayed human remains that he had been mentally preparing for. *Didn't it?*

"What have you found?" Hoa asked in Vietnamese. The old woman was leaning over the hole, with her hands held up to her eyes, shielding them from the glare of the sun.

Ricky responded to her, then repeated himself in English. "Nothing. Just a box."

Hoa seemed crestfallen, her shoulders slumped with disappointment as though it had suddenly hit her that she would never find her brother and release him from his supposed fate. She stood in silence with the two girls on one side of her and Ali on the other, unable to make sense of the situation. Hector wanted to say something, to share some words of sympathy, but nothing he could think of seemed right. Instead, he kept his head down and helped Ricky scoop out the mud around the rusted edges bit by bit.

After another ten minutes, they were deep enough to ease the case out of the ground. Patches of peeling green paint, among the oxidised metal and dirt, were the only specks that hinted at its original colour. A small, rusted-through padlock kept the box closed.

Wanting to make sure he captured the atmosphere of the search, Hector scrambled out of the ditch and paced over to his camera bag, rubbing the soil off his hands onto his jeans as he went. While Ricky worked the container free, he took a few shots, making sure to catch the group standing over the hole, with mixed expressions of sadness, intrigue, and excitement on their faces. Apart from the click of Hector's shutter, there was silence. Even the forest seemed to have quietened around them as if waiting for the grand reveal.

Ricky worked the box side to side until it came loose and heaved it out onto the soil. He gave the lock a sharp tug and the degraded metal broke immediately. He discarded it on the ground at his side.

The five figures gathered round the box, tense like a coiled spring as their guide slowly lifted the lid, and an expression of awe crossed his face.

"Well?" Em said, obviously unable to bear the anticipation any better than Hector.

Ricky dropped the box top back to reveal its contents. A long-barrelled automatic pistol. At its side, a crumbling cardboard box of bullets and a small, rough-spun hessian bag tied closed with a string.

"Jesus," Hector said. "Do you think it's still functional?" The weapon appeared to be in pretty decent condition, not obviously rusted or decayed, considering someone had probably buried it the best part of half a century ago.

Ricky inspected the gun. "Looks like it," he said. Then he picked up the bag, pulled open the knot with his long fingernails and emptied the contents onto his muddy palm. Ten tarnished gold coins dropped out, glinting in the sunlight, each one seeming to be marked with some type of Chinese character.

"Holy shit!" Ali squawked. "That's some serious cash."

Ricky shook his head, glimpsing Ali's eyes wide with excitement. He dropped the coins back in the bag and pulled the strings shut. Silently, their guide closed the case. He rose to his feet and turned to Hoa, who still stood shaking as she watched over the proceedings. He lifted her hand and dropped the bag onto her palm.

"They belong to you," he said, first in her native language, then in English.

With mixed emotions overwhelming her, the old woman started to cry. Tears ran down her weathered cheeks and pooled in the loose skin at the pit of her neck.

As everyone gathered around Hoa, offering her their condolences, Ali stepped down into the pit, lifting the lid off the box and picked up the gun.

"Fucking outstanding," he muttered, pointed it into the forest and squeezed the trigger. Realising a moment too late that he was about to shoot, Hector clamped his eyes shut in a knee-jerk reaction. A metallic clunk rang out, and the group let out a collective sigh of relief.

"Put that back," Anna said in a scolding tone like she was talking to a rebellious child.

"Alright, keep your wig on. Just wanted to see if it still worked. Looks like it does."

"How would you know?" Hector asked. "Just because it fired unloaded doesn't actually mean it would shoot a bullet."

"Yeah, but if it does, it'd be worth loads more."

"Mate, you can't take any of this stuff. I thought Ricky made that clear. We're here to observe only."

"That's bullshit!" he said. "She's down to take a fucking literal bag of gold and I'm not even allowed a handgun as a souvenir?"

"That's right," Anna answered. "Hoa has a right to the gold. You have no claim to anything whatsoever. We need to put that back and bury it again. It's bad luck to even handle something that has taken a life."

Ali looked like he was about to fight it, but Em slid in front of him and wrapped her arms round his neck. "Don't worry, babe, you can claim me instead."

His frown melted into a filthy grin. "Okay, darling, but that means I gotta plant my flagpole in you."

She smirked, offering neither a yes nor a no. "For now, though, be a good boy and put the gun back."

"Alright."

Hector, Ricky, and Anna walked Hoa over to the shade and sat her down, still looking badly shaken. While they did their best to keep her calm, Ali picked up the box. He rattled the bullets around for a moment, then slid the handgun into the front of his waistband and concealed it under his vest. The Australian closed the lid and lowered the container back into the hole, then half-heartedly kicked a pile of dirt over the top.

Chapter Thirteen

Day One
16:18
Present Day

The group probably could have kept digging, but they all knew it wasn't leading anywhere. The trench was almost three feet deep and covered most of the clearing. If Hoa's brother was to be found, it wasn't here.

The sun was already growing heavy in the sky, and, although it wouldn't set for another couple of hours, Hector had learned that night fell fast in this part of the world. The dark had already caught him and Ali off guard a few times during this trip. One moment they'd been cruising through the countryside, enjoying the warm rays of sunset, and the next, they suddenly found themselves driving on near-lethal mountain roads in the pitch-black.

The only thing the group could do now was to head back to camp, where they could further examine Hoa's instructions, hoping to find where they went wrong today.

Almost an hour passed before the group got close enough to see the distant shimmer of the water. Red rays of late-afternoon sunlight stretched through the trees, their glow punctuated by dark patches of forest and bubbles of cool air that the sun never touched.

Another narrow track joined their path from the western side of the island. It looked like some kind of animal trail. But whatever creature had made it certainly wasn't small.

"You guys go ahead," Ricky said, dropping back from the front of the column as they continued down the path that led to the waterfront.

"What about you?" Em asked, as Ricky backtracked to where she and Ali were once again bringing up the rear.

"I'm going to step outside. Best not to be too close to camp."

"We're already outside, mate. Literally in the middle of a fucking forest," Ali replied.

"It's a euphemism," Anna said, turning back towards him.

After a long hot day, Ali's sense of humour was starting to wear thin on most of them.

"Ricky was politely saying he's going to take a shit. Although, I guess subtlety isn't your strong suit."

Hector laughed, looking over his shoulder and catching her eye.

"Fuckin' right it's not."

The group carried on for another few minutes before the green and black canvas of the tents finally became visible at the lakeside.

Hector and Hoa settled on logs around the still-glowing embers that remained of the fire. Ali disappeared for a minute and returned with his backpack. He fished out a couple of cans of 333 that were hot to the touch after spending all afternoon in the sweltering tent. He dropped one on Hector's lap and held another up for Hoa, saying, "*Bia?*" However, she didn't even seem to notice.

The old woman sat pensively, running the bag's string through her fingers and feeling the weight of the pouch. She looked uncertain whether the coins were a blessing or a curse.

The girls both ventured into Anna's tent. Based on the sounds of the rustling bags and zips, they were probably changing clothes.

As the two men drank their warm beers, Hector flicked through the images on his camera. Despite the failure of the dig, he was growing more and more confident that he'd have one hell of a story to tell at the end of the trip. *Maybe I should just write what I care about and to hell with anyone who doesn't like it?*

"That was a pretty cool afternoon," Ali said.

"Yeah, it was. I feel bad for Hoa though. She's been waiting twenty years for today. She really believed she was going to find him too, didn't she?"

"Well, yeah." Ali glanced over his shoulder at the old woman, half expecting her to react, but she didn't so much as move. "Still, though, you don't need to feel that bad for her. She could always try again. I mean, she found a godda—"

A piercing scream rang out through the trees, cutting Ali off. The sound was harsh and desperate, filled with either great pain or fear. Hector leapt to his feet and Ali followed suit.

"What in fuck's name was that?"

Hector searched for an explanation but came up with nothing. Besides the six of them, there wasn't another soul on the island that they knew of, at least. Anna bundled out of the tent, with Em a moment behind her. "What was that noise?"

"Sounded like Ricky. He must have hurt himself," Hector said. "You guys stay here. Ali and I will find him. Give me your phone number in case we need to call you."

"Errm, sure. Yeah, okay," Anna replied, sounding flustered. She reeled off the nine-digit number while Hector tapped it into his dirt-cheap Nokia, blissfully unaware that they both had no service.

He slung his camera bag inside the tent that he and Ricky were due to be sharing and set off with Ali back into the forest quickly.

"Smooth move getting her number," Ali said as he broke into a half jog.

"I was thinking about safety," Hector muttered back. "Not everything is about sex." Ali's attitude was starting to grate a little on him as well.

They soon came to the part of the path that joined up with the animal track, near where Ricky had split off.

"He's got to be round here. RICKY!" Hector shouted, cupping his hands to his mouth. "Where are you?"

They waited a few seconds. *No answer.* A sinking feeling swelled in Hector's stomach. Their guide must really be hurt. *Maybe he's slipped and broken something or hit his head?* Although, neither of those reasons would explain his silence. *It must be bad.*

"We need to split up," he told Ali. "You go left, I'll go right. Meet back at this spot in ten minutes. And try to remember which way you're going."

"Yeah, yeah," Ali replied dismissively.

The Australian had got them lost enough times so far on this trip for Hector to know how poor his sense of direction was. "Really. Keep an eye out, please?"

"Okay." Ali nodded, without some glib remark for once. *Maybe he can actually take some things seriously after all.*

Hector ventured off into the trees on the right, following the path of least resistance, looking for what must have seemed like a suitable spot to shit. Only two minutes went by before Ali shouted back.

"I've found him. Over here." The Australian's voice was fearful and squeaky, sounding a world away from the man he'd been just moments before.

Hector bolted back towards the path, ignoring the finger-like branches that scratched at every inch of his exposed skin.

As Ali emerged from the shadowy treeline before him, his face was white as a ghost.

"Where is he?" Hector asked.

His friend turned and pointed at the gap in the trees without a word.

"Oh my god."

Chapter Fourteen

Day One
17:45
Present Day

From Hector's position thirty feet away, there was no way for him to mistake the shiny gold and black patterns of Ricky's shirt from where he lay on the floor.

As Hector pushed past Ali, who stood frozen on the spot, the reason for his friend's sudden change in demeanour became apparent. Ricky was lying face down in the leaves with red tendrils of blood snaking out onto the dirt from underneath him.

Hector dashed the last few feet and skidded onto his knees amongst the bloodied leaves and topsoil. Ali stepped up behind, the confidence all but drained from his usual swagger.

With one hand on their guide's shoulder, Hector rocked Ricky's body forward and back, attempting to roll him over, while instinctively trying to avoid getting covered in the young man's blood. It took more effort than he expected to move the dead weight, but when he finally got Ricky over onto his back, the sight of his horrific wounds soon made Hector forget everything else.

Across Ricky's front were more than half a dozen deep stab wounds. Each messy and torn, oozing thick purple-black blood. But against all odds, Ricky was still breathing, his chest rising and falling slightly in a fast, sporadic rhythm. Each inhale produced a raspy, wet wheezing sound, like someone was trying to blow up a soaking wet balloon.

"Shit! We need to get help."

"How?" Ali's voice shuddered.

"I dunno. We have to call someone... An ambulance, a helicopter, or something to get him to a hospital. Anything!"

The Australian was staring blankly into the trees. His face looked haunted in the twilight.

"ALI!" Hector shouted, and the other man snapped back to reality. "Run back, get the girls to call the emergency services. Then bring them here. We're gonna need help lifting him. I'll try to keep pressure on the wounds. Bring a bunch of clothes so that I can make some kind of tourniquet. Oh, and your vodka, so we can clean them."

"Okay," Ali said again, this time with a little more conviction.

"Don't just fucking stand there then. GO!"

Ali spun on his heels and rushed back into the forest the way they'd come. Hector's hands were shaking violently as he pushed down on Ricky's chest, covering the worst of the wounds and trying to hold back the sickeningly warm flow.

Their guide's weakening convulsions made Hector certain he was doing the completely wrong thing. He needed a better way to stem the bleeding. *Please don't get lost, Ali.*

The next few minutes seemed like an eternity as Hector felt each one of the young man's breaths become more and more laboured. The look in Ricky's eyes was distant and glassy, as though he no longer knew where he was or why.

Hector had read plenty of stories about war and survival. From them, he'd learned that there were two types of people, each of which would only reveal their true nature under duress. One, those who panicked and fell to pieces, and the other, those who kept their head and drew focus from the fear.

It was more than a little surprising for Hector to find out he was the latter. He'd never done well with blood in real life, but fortunately, adrenaline seemed to narrow his thoughts and fix him on the task at hand—keeping Ricky alive.

Despite his best efforts, by the time Ali burst back through the trees with Em and Anna close in tow, the strained breaths had stopped completely. All the colour had drained from Ricky's face, leaving his skin a revolting shade of beige.

As the adrenaline had faded, a wave of overwhelming exhaustion left Hector slumped beside the body, holding up his head in bloodied palms.

Em was first into the clearing behind Ali. She screamed on seeing the body and immediately threw up in the bushes at her side, but Hector barely heard the sounds of her retching. Anna froze, her eyes wide, trying to come to terms with what she was seeing.

"What happened?" she finally asked, her voice sombre, as she pushed through the others.

"He's... dead." Hector had known this for the last few minutes but had been trying not to believe it. Somehow, by saying it out loud, he made the horrific fact real. Tears streamed down his face.

A minute later, Hoa came lumbering through the bushes. Anna spun on the spot, stopping the old woman from coming any closer.

Em wiped her mouth with the back of her hand. "How did this happen?" she asked, her voice trembling.

Hector had been so consumed by trying to save Ricky's life, he hadn't even thought about the morbid circumstances of his wounds. *This was obviously no accident*, he realised, hit by a fresh wave of nausea. There were a dozen vicious stab wounds across Ricky's torso. It was a fast, brutal attack without mercy. *But why? Who? And where are they now?*

Hoa was on her knees praying for the next ten minutes while the rest of the group stood around her with ashen faces and sunken eyes. Finally, the old woman rose to her feet. She spoke a few words to Anna so quietly they were almost inaudible.

Hoa's voice was calm and solid. This was definitely not the first body she had seen, unlike the youngsters who were all shaken to their core. "We need to cover him," Anna translated. "It'll help protect his spirit until we can take him back home. Have we got anything to lie across his body?"

This Hector could do, a simple practical task that he hoped would both take his mind off the murder and put the body out of sight. Although, he had a feeling that he was going to be seeing Ricky's cold, dead face every time he closed his eyes anyway. "Let's use one of the tents' outer covers. I'll take one from the camp," he said and turned to leave.

"Wait, I'll come too," Anna said. "You shouldn't go off alone, not with whoever did *this* still out there."

"Good point." Between the shock of Ricky's death and his desire to put some distance between himself and the corpse, Hector had obviously not been thinking straight.

Anna turned back to Em and Ali. "Can you two stay here with Hoa?"

"Yes," the model answered solemnly. From the look on her face, Em seemed to be realising for the very first time that she was, in fact, not the centre of the universe.

Hector led the way. He and Anna paced quickly through the near-dark forest as though speed was still important.

It wasn't long before they made it back to camp. The pair unclipped and pulled off the thick outer layer from the tent to the right of the hut. Ricky's tent.

"We need torches," Anna said. "It'll be pitch-black in a few minutes."

"Good idea," Hector answered, his first words since they'd set off.

Anna fished around in her and Hoa's tent until she found one. Meanwhile, he went into Ali's tent and rifled through his friend's bag, soon finding what he was looking for. Ali was utterly useless at answering calls or messages. Most of the time, he seemed to forget he even had a phone.

Hector tapped the screen, bringing the device to life. *Damn.* Just as he expected, it had absolutely no signal. Still, the phone could be another light source for now. *Maybe there'll be reception elsewhere on the island.*

He then went over to the remaining interior of the tent he and Ricky were supposed to be sharing, unzipped the white netting, and climbed inside.

The camera bag was sitting in the corner. Hector looked at it for a moment then decided against picking it up and moved to the other side. The image of Ricky's dying body was one he'd rather never have to look upon again, even though taking a few photos for evidence was certainly a good idea.

Tucked neatly in the left-hand corner was Ricky's red hiking backpack. Hector recalled the head torch he'd seen the guide drop inside when he'd been arguing with his mum the night before. It felt like weeks ago now.

Rooting around in the bag, Hector pushed past piles of supplies bundled up in military-style canvas wraps. At the bottom, his hand found the circular plastic outline of the torch and tugged it up, but the elastic bands had become wrapped around something. Not wanting to take everything out, he fumbled trying to release the device, to no avail.

"Fucking thing," Hector shouted in frustration, losing complete control of his emotions for no good reason.

He wrenched as hard as he could, finally pulling the torch, among other things, free from their bindings. He panted for a moment, fighting the rising wave of panic triggered by something so mundane.

After a few seconds, he calmed down and adjusted the elastic straps. They'd obviously been set up to fit someone much smaller than him. Hector ran his fingers over its body until he found a soft rubber button and the sterile white glow of three high-powered LEDs filled the tiny canvas pyramid, revealing an array of Ricky's possessions, now scattered across the floor.

"Are you ready to go yet?" Anna called, sounding nervous, and stuck her head into the tent. Her gaze immediately flicked down to the mess of items on the groundsheet. One of which was a garish T-shirt, streaked with luminous green and pink tribal patterns on white—something that would have looked at home in Ibiza in the mid-1990s. It was obviously not Hector's.

"Oh my God, what are you doing?" Anna's eyes bulged. "Ricky hasn't even been dead an hour and you're already looting his stuff?"

Hector hadn't even considered how this might look to her. More worrying was the fact that their guide had just been murdered, with only him and Ali finding the body.

"Did you and your psycho friend kill him? Is this about the gold?!"

Hector's heart was galloping like the bass drum at an Iron Maiden stadium gig. He took a slow breath and prayed his words wouldn't desert him. He'd always been able to explain himself convincingly. The only issue was, this ability usually came a few hours or even days after he needed it. That was why, he thought, he was a much better writer than he was a speaker.

"No! Of course not. I needed his torch. Ricky didn't even have the gold. Besides, we were here the whole time, weren't we? You can ask Hoa."

A flash of realisation that he wasn't lying sparked in Anna's eyes. "You're right. I'm sorry, that was stupid of me."

"It's okay." He couldn't fault her for being paranoid. The only reason *he* wasn't blaming Ricky's death on one of the others was because he had been with all four of them at the time. *Hadn't he?*

Suspicion stewed in Hector's mind for a few seconds before he dismissed it as madness. Ali had always been wild and impulsive, but he wasn't a psychopath. Hector was *pretty* sure of that, at least. Likewise, neither Em nor Anna would have had the physical strength to do such damage. It's not like any of them had a motive. *Did they?*

"Either way, we need to be careful. Ricky was obviously mixed up in something terrible. We just need to make sure that we're not implicated in this."

"Us? Why would we be?"

"Maybe because we paid him to take us to a deserted island, used him to locate a bunch of gold coins, and then found him murdered an hour later."

She nodded, understanding a little where he was coming from, if not entirely. Hector knew he'd probably been watching too many crime dramas for his own good, but as an outsider in a Communist country, it was reasonable that he would be overly concerned. For Anna though, this was her country, these were her people. *Surely, she and Em will vouch for us if the worse comes to worst?*

"Let's just get the tent sheet over there and cover Ricky up, then try to find our way off this goddamn island." The thought of spending the night alongside a corpse in the jungle, with a killer on the loose, sent a sickening chill down Hector's spine.

Arcs of white LED light cut through the trees, sending nocturnal creatures scurrying in fear, while swarms of moths and mosquitoes clouded them with a blanket of grey-brown wings.

It was slow progress. Each bend in the path or tree along the way that Hector thought he could remember now seemed to be absent. Instead, he only saw imagined figures looming in the darkness, and *real* glowing eyes staring back at them from the trees. Both he and Anna were desperately on edge.

Finally, after almost triple the time it had taken them to get back to camp, the pair emerged into the grove. At an almost-respectful distance from Ricky's body, Ali was lying on top of a fallen log with his eyes closed. Hoa was sitting on another stump, staring into space, her features looking gaunt and tired.

Anna led the way, with Hector behind her. Together, they dragged the sheet forward and let it drop to the ground a few feet from where the corpse lay.

Ali shielded his eyes as the bright light dazzled him. "Jesus, that took you a fuckin' while." At least he sounded like himself again. A small smile broke through Hector's lips until the reason for his trip sprang back to the forefront of his mind.

"It was hard to find the way."

"Where's Em?" Anna said.

Hoa looked up on hearing the girl's name and glanced around. Ali rolled his head over towards Hector and Anna. "Dunno. She was here a minute ago."

"Em?" Anna called, the worry in her voice unmistakable.

The exact same thought had been on Hector's mind, a sick, sinking feeling growing in his gut. "EM?"

No answer came. "We have to find her," Anna said. "Right now,"

Hector nodded. "Let's make two pairs. Ali, you and Hoa go left, me and Anna will go right, then we'll meet back here."

"Relax," Ali answered. "She can't have gone far. Probably 'stepped outside' too," he said with a smirk.

"For fuck's sake, man," Hector burst out. "We were only gone a few minutes. How could you be so irresponsible?"

"Hey. Don't put that shit on me. Maybe you should just admit you made a goddamn mistake talking us all into coming here rather than blaming it on someone else!"

"Can I remind you both that a man is dead and my best friend is missing?" Anna looked like she was about to smack one of them in the face. "This is not the time for petty squabbles."

"Sorry. You're right. Let's go find her."

This turned out to be a task much easier said than done.

Chapter Fifteen

Day One
21:04
Fifty Years Ago

"GET OFF THE PATH!" The squad leader's roar echoed through Sang's mind. When it had actually taken place more than a year before, his scream had been lost beneath the sudden thunder of rotor blades. However, in the memories that Sang relived nightly, it still sounded clear as day.

She closed her eyes and it was as though she was back there, diving from the dike into the black waters of the rice paddy. They glimmered like polished obsidian beneath her, lit by the glow of a full moon.

Sang crashed through the surface. Murky, stagnant liquid filled her throat and nose as she sank. Meanwhile, a white spotlight—nearly as bright as the summer sun—swept across the valley above her.

Clasping at the roots of young plants on the bottom of the waterlogged field, Sang fought for grip. Fortunately, the weight of her sodden combat fatigues and the heavy load on her back were enough to keep her submerged in the shallow rice paddy.

Her head started to spin. Every cell in her body was screaming for oxygen as she waited in desperation for the roar of rotor blades to soften. An instant before she took a lungful of water, Sang burst up through the surface.

Two figures, fifty feet ahead, had emerged seconds before, both soaked and panting. The closest was Kien, a private from Thanh Hoa Province, who was always smiling and laughing. She could tell by his backpack, he always kept his machete strapped on to the top. Through the plants and distorted light, she couldn't make out front-most man.

Kien turned and caught Sang's eye as if to say, "we made it". Unbeknown to him, the American Huey gunship was swooping round to his rear. She went to shout a warning but choked, paralysed with fear.

The chopper streamed towards them like an eagle diving for fish from the lake. Its side-mounted machine gun spun to life. The volume was deafening as a hundred metal shafts slammed into the paddy like a pounding summer rain of white-hot lead.

Heavy fire shredded Kien and the other soldier in a flash, throwing a tempestuous cloud of blood and stagnant water into the air.

Pure, visceral fear forced Sang back into the blackened waters. Even below the surface, the sheer volume of the gunfire sent her senses into overload. She was sure that this was the end.

Eventually, the shooting stopped and the spotlights faded. When Sang finally emerged again, it was to a sense of utter mayhem. Between the ringing in her head, water-logged ears, and flares of light burnt into her retinas, the confusion was overwhelming.

Sang pulled her body out onto dry ground and wiped the tears from her face, only to find her hands came away covered in blood. The taste was on her lips and in her throat too. She retched and searched her shaking body for the source. It wasn't long before she realised that the water in which she had hidden was now entirely red.

Desperate to find anyone still alive, Sang waded back into the paddy, calling for her friends.

All she found of Kien was a bullet-riddled bag, still with his machete tied across the top. The guilt of knowing she could have saved his life with a mere shout, but didn't, felt like icy fingers tightening around her throat.

When the few remaining men from Unit Sixty-Six found Sang, she was still stood in waist-deep water, gripping Kien's bag and staring blankly into the distance. She had no idea how much time had passed.

Sang shook herself from the daze, her traumatised mind slowly returning to here and now. *You can't let them down again,* she thought, instinctively tightening her embrace around Ly.

After Truong had explained to the poor child why her father wasn't coming back, Ly had eventually cried herself to sleep. At least in her dreams, she might still be with her family.

Sang ground her teeth so hard she could taste the calcium in her throat. She didn't know whether it was vengeance, redemption, or hope she so desperately craved, but she was certain about one thing. It would be a cold day in hell before she just sat here and did nothing but wait for her husband to meet the same fate as Private Nam.

Why hasn't he returned yet? A voice somewhere in the back of Sang's head whispered in response. *You need to find your husband. Then kill your enemies before they kill you.*

Sang laid Ly down on her bed and kissed the little girl on the cheek. She silently slipped into the jacket of her military fatigues, and picked up the long, white candle that burned beside her bunk. The uniform hung off Sang's frame; she'd lost most of her curves after a year of eating cardboard-like military rations every day. Regardless, it would keep her warm and hidden. That was all that mattered.

Huy was awake, sitting cross-legged on his bunk in the corner, mouthing words to himself as if singing a song, but never made a sound. Captain Chien, Khai, and Grandma Lan were all fast asleep.

The mute veteran watched Sang go, but it wasn't like he was going to tell everyone. Besides, she was a soldier now—whether Truong liked it or not—and no one would stop her from doing her duty.

Crossing the darkened cavern was a challenge in itself. Sang's candle threw bizarre, twisted shapes all around as it carved out a bubble of light in the shadows.

On the northern wall, she found the familiar cold metal of the supply rack and slid *Ares*, her Kalashnikov, off the wall.

Sang slipped out the thirty-round magazine to make sure it was full, then manually cocked the weapon and pulled the trigger twice. A hollow click echoed in the ghostly cavern, proving, as she expected, that it hadn't succumbed to the damp conditions.

She'd heard tales that the American guns needed only a few drops of moisture to get inside for them to seize up completely. In comparison, *Ares*, designed by her Soviet comrades and built with hardy Chinese steel, seemed virtually indestructible.

She reloaded the magazine and followed the wall, running her fingers across the wet, ridged stone until the volume of the river grew loud enough to tell her she had arrived.

Truong had given the order not to turn the mining lamps on again tonight. The decision was obviously tactical. He wanted to ensure that if he and Long didn't make it back, any potential attackers' progress on the outpost would be as slow as possible.

With a hand on the string of the extinguished lamps, Sang guided herself into the tunnel. It reminded her of a French book from her father's library. As a girl, she'd been enthralled by the tale of Scott's expedition to the Antarctic, having never seen snow herself. When it was too white to see, the explorers would set up ropes between each station so feel alone could guide them. To her misguided adolescent mind, the danger faced by the Antarctic explorers had seemed exciting and romantic. A far cry from the realities of war.

Sang ducked and weaved to avoid enormous dripping stalactites, then crawled beneath low-jutting rocks. The awkward shape of the tunnel made carrying supplies in and out of the cavern a challenge. It often took a fully equipped unit the better part of an hour. However, with nothing more than Ares on her back, Sang reached the entrance in less than a third of that.

She slipped out through the narrow passageway, pushing aside the hanging vines and bushes. Without knowing exactly where to look, especially under cover of darkness, the entrance to the cave was virtually impossible to see.

For the first time in nearly a month, Sang took a lungful of fresh air and set her eyes on the sky. The light of a full moon cracked through heavy summer rain clouds. They were swollen and bulbous, threatening, but not yet overdue. A few of the brighter stars seemed to dance like fireflies through the gaps in the overcast sky. Only then did she realise how much she had missed it.

Somewhere in the distance, thunder rumbled, accompanied by distant flashes high in the atmosphere. She had a tarpaulin and a hammock in her bag just in case, but right now, rain was the least of her worries.

Keeping her body tight to the mountain wall, Sang moved west, being careful to avoid the crescent of dugout tiger traps that surrounded the entrance.

These pits were lined with sharpened bamboo stakes, designed to slow down a squad by injuring rather than killing. However, falling into one without someone to help you back out would make for a very slow and painful death. Luckily, Sang's night vision was sharp as a knife, and she could easily pick out the false floors.

As she headed away from the rocky face of the mountain, down the sloping path to the west, the forest came alive around her. It was humming with the croak of cicadas, while the nocturnal rodents—no bigger than her thumb—rustled as they fled at the sound of human footsteps.

The air was damp and musty, but the warmth of it made her feel regenerated. Even the sour aroma of rotting fruit on the ground brought a smile to her face, reminding her of simpler days.

There was no direct trail up to the caves, as Truong and his men would vary their routes in and out of the outpost, making sure they left no obvious markings. So Sang simply followed the path of least resistance for a long while. With each step she took further into the night, her hope grew further. Truong was a survivor, like her. *He's still alive,* she told herself, *and he needs me.*

Chapter Sixteen

Day One
21:06
Present Day

After nearly an hour of walking endless loops around the area, calling Em's name, and jumping at shadows, Anna looked as though she was on the verge of a panic attack. No doubt running different scenarios through her head, as the fruitless search grew more and more bleak.

Finally, Hector called it, deciding the group should head back to the camp. Maybe it was a fool's hope, but there was always a chance that the fashionista had got lost and wandered back there looking for them.

As they walked, Hector did his best to keep Anna grounded, reassuring her that Em was safe, even though he harboured his own powerful doubts. As they trudged, he realised it was time to embrace the feeling he'd had since the first moment he'd set eyes on the island. What it was exactly, he couldn't quite tell, but something about this place felt *wrong*.

By the time they reached the main stretch of path leading to the camp, Hoa looked dead on her feet. The old woman needed to rest and refuel, or they might well find another corpse in their midst.

Ali and Anna walked beside Hoa along the narrow trail, doing their best to support her with one shoulder each. All the while, Anna scanned the darkness, hoping to glimpse her friend in the shadows. Or maybe hoping not to, for fear of what she might find. At the front, Hector led the way with the bright LEDs on his head.

"Wait!" he whispered back over his shoulder, raising an open hand, and the group froze. "What was that?"

Hector held his breath until he was sure the only sounds were the scratching of insects at their feet and faint rustles in the high treetops overhead. He eventually breathed a sigh of relief, despite swearing that there had been voices somewhere in the distance.

Just as he was cursing his own wild imagination, the noise came again. A gruff voice, harsh and angry, floated through the forest. Hector spun on his heels, locking eyes with Ali, fearful to confirm what he'd heard.

"Who the fuck was that?" The Australian's eyes were almost popping from his head.

"Turn the lights off quick."

Hector flicked the switch on his head torch, and Anna covered the beam of hers with an open hand, plunging them into absolute darkness. Only then, a slight orange glow became apparent through the trees. The camp was ablaze.

A sudden change in the wind brought the smell of plastic-fuelled smoke and something much worse. The voice from before was now accompanied by a desperate whimpering sound.

"Em!" Anna said, sliding out from under Hoa's arm and breaking into a sprint towards the light over the darkened trail.

Hector quickly blocked her path, grabbing Anna's wrist. "Wait," he hissed. "I know you're worried for Em, but we have no idea who's over there or why." The look in her eyes was one of desperation and anger, but she knew he was right. "At least let me and Ali go first and check it out."

There was a killer on the loose. The two men, Ali in particular, who stood at six foot four and was close to two hundred and twenty pounds of muscle, would undoubtedly fare better in a hostile encounter than the petite young woman.

"Please don't let anything happen to my friend," Anna pleaded, tears balling up in the corners of her eyes.

Hector put a hand on her shoulder, wanting to give her a hug and make her feel safe, but resisted the urge. Now wasn't the time. "Em'll be fine. I promise. Stay here and keep Hoa safe, and we'll be back soon."

The old woman started whispering fast, as she realised what they were going to do.

"What's she complaining about?" Ali asked, keeping his voice low.

"Hoa thinks we're cursed because of the gold. She wants you to take it with you and give it back somehow."

That wasn't a bad idea. Even if it was just blind superstition, maybe they could bargain with whoever it was on the island with them. *Maybe that'll be enough to keep us safe?*

Hector took the pouch from the old lady, offering a quick bow of his head. He had to at least make it seem like he was taking her idea seriously.

In darkness, the two men crept forward. Fifty feet from the camp, thick, black fumes from burning canvas and plastic filled the forest, making Hector's eyes stream with tears and his throat sting with every breath. A double whammy of frustration then hit as he realised his camera, and the only actual evidence for what they were doing on the island in the first place, was probably smouldering among the ruins of the camp.

Pushing through the haze, the voices soon became more distinct. There were at least two men and a woman, all speaking in English, but the words were too low and distant to make any out clearly. Hector started to second guess his eagerness to look brave in front of Anna. He was definitely a lover, not a fighter.

The pair moved off the trail and crept through the trees, deliberately approaching the hut in the shadows, hoping to remain unseen. Tangles of roots and sharp rocks covered the ground, making progress even more sluggish, but they couldn't risk moving any faster and giving themselves away with a trip or a fall.

Twenty feet from the right-hand side of the hut, Hector got his first look at the source of the noise. The door was ajar, a fire was burning within, on the same spot the charred wood had been earlier. Whereas outside, the flames had more-or-less petered out, and the wreck of the camp was now smouldering and smoking.

With his heart pounding, Hector crept further round the perimeter until his worst fears were confirmed. Em came into view. She was kneeling, facing into the hut. From this angle, he could only make out the bottom of her legs and part of her back. He recognised the bright-blue tattoo of a butterfly on her calf straight away. It was definitely her. Beyond that, the door and the far wall blocked his vision.

A breeze blew through the camp, carrying in not only the scent of smoke but something far worse. The odour was like putrid rotting meat.

"What can you see, mate?" Ali whispered from the rear, his view obscured behind Hector. It was probably a blessing in disguise, knowing Ali, he'd charge in there with reckless abandon. He had a good heart, but certainly didn't always make the best decisions.

"She's in there."

"Lucky, I still got this fucker then," Ali said. From the front of his shorts, he slipped out the semi-automatic pistol they had found alongside the gold and quietly cocked the weapon.

"When the hell did you take that?" Hector whispered, unsure if he was furious or over the moon. Maybe some leverage would be good?

"I lied about putting it back, and I bet you're glad I did."

"Does it even work?"

"Fuck knows." Ali slid a handful of bullets from his pocket, released the cartridge, thumbed them in one by one, and reloaded.

"Just don't do anything crazy, okay? We're gonna be in deep enough shit as it is."

"Yeah, yeah. It's only for a bit of insurance anyway. They won't fuck with us if they know we're packing heat."

Hector shook his head. *Jesus Christ, this escalated quickly.*

The pair edged further around the trees until they were at the far side of the camp, hidden among the branches, with the lake to their right. In the flickering firelight, Hector saw Em properly for the first time. She was sobbing, her face streaked with mascara-stained tears.

A bubble of rage swelled in Hector's chest as he laid eyes on the man standing over Em, even though he could only see his back.

The captor wasn't particularly tall, but he was built like a tank, with shoulders almost the same size as Ali's. He had a short blonde buzz cut and was wearing a dark-green outfit. The bottom half of his clothes were torn and patched with something black that looked like mud.

"Let's try this another way then, shall we?" the blonde man said. His accent was American, a thick southern drawl of Alabama or Tennessee — somewhere deep south. *What the hell is he doing here?*

Em's captor stepped forward casually, right up in front of her, and stood fumbling with something for a moment. Only then did Hector realise the blonde man had taken his cock out.

"Please? Don't make me," Em begged.

"Put. It. In. Your. Mouth."

"NO!" she shouted through her tears. The blonde man, still with his cock out, exploded forward with his knee. It slammed into Em's face, sending shards of teeth and splatters of blood across the floor. She hit the ground, whimpering in fear a moment later.

"Hey Truman," the blonde man said. "This ain't gonna do much good for that pretty face now, is it?"

A second man stepped forward, also dressed in what looked like military fatigues. He was taller and wiry with short, black hair. Truman clicked his tongue in derision and laughed.

"No, sir, it isn't." His voice was rougher. Hector figured it was maybe a New York or a Boston accent, somewhere round there. "In fact, I don't think she'll be sucking anything for a while."

"MOTHERFUCKER!" Ali exploded, and before Hector could even react, he burst from the trees, running towards the structure with the gun drawn.

The Australian cleared ten feet before the men in the hut spun to face him. Ali's legs locked up. He skidded in the dirt and ash as if he had run into a wall of glass and dropped the gun. *Oh My God.*

Chapter Seventeen

Day One
22:18
Present Day

"STAND DOWN!" the blonde soldier bellowed, whipping a huge silver revolver from his belt and taking aim at Ali.

The second man, the one he had called Truman, spun round, pulling his gun up to his shoulder. While two more figures moved from the shadows at the rear of the hut, both drawing weapons.

Ali skidded back through the dirt on his hands, trying to put some distance between him and the soldiers. He accidentally kicked the gun he'd dropped with his heel until they were both just five feet from the treeline.

Hector's jaw almost hit the floor as the monstrous crew emerged into full view. The leader's skin was a sickly grey colour. The right side of his face was concave, with a deep hole where his eye should have been. It was thick with dried blood and yellow, infected flesh, eventually giving way to a black mess of burnt gristle and bone in the centre. Dried blood covered the entire bottom half of the leader's torso and the material beneath his groin was a torn and tattered mess. Hector's stomach clenched and hot, acidic bile rose up into his throat. The only saving grace was that the soldier had put away whatever remained of his penis before he turned.

Truman stood behind his leader, aiming down the barrel of a very large automatic machine gun. He was a gangly man, with dark hair and beady eyes. A hole in his face showed a grim exposed cheek bone and a cream-coloured layer of cartilage beneath. However, the more devastating wounds seemed to be the several bullet holes that perforated his chest.

At the rear, a third figure edged forward. He had a tightly shorn Afro and a few days' worth of black stubble. His nose was badly broken and patches of burnt skin were peeling off his face. The soldier was covered in dust, with shards of rusty, pointed metal sticking out of his neck and chest.

The lower Hector looked, the fouler and more foetid the embedded fragments seemed to become. The final shard, an inch above the bladder, oozed thick black paste. Without a doubt, these wounds were the source of the repugnant odour that he had smelled earlier.

Finally, at the far back and still struggling with his weapon, was the youngest of the group. The man was skinny and frail looking. His face, torso, and legs were covered with dozens of rust-coloured puncture wounds, each one the size of a penny.

All four men sported names over their right breasts. RICKARD, HIGGS, TRUMAN and WATTS. Rickard had three inverted Vs on his right arm over a pair of crossed rifles—a sergeant. Truman bore a double V, while the other man wore a single stripe, denoting his rank as a private. Hector knew that much about military insignia, at least. The youngest of the group was Watts, who had a single blue pair of wings above his name, setting him apart from the three marines. *The interpreter*, Hector realised.

Without a doubt, they were the special-ops squad from the report Hector had read. Somehow, despite all of them being deceased, the Americans were up and walking around, hunting, interrogating, and raping, as if to spit in the face of all that is holy.

Hector couldn't breathe. The damp forest air, heavy with burnt carbon and the stench of death, was choking. He stumbled backwards until his shoulder smacked into a nearby trunk and he leaned against it, gasping for air.

Just like that, every sceptical opinion, every logical argument he'd ever made about the paranormal or the afterlife was kicked in the balls, smashed in the teeth, and pushed out the window. If he'd been wrong about something as huge as this, what else might he have been wrong about? Despite the horrific scene before him, a sense of utter foolishness prevailed.

"Hold it right there," Sergeant Rickard growled. A mixture of black, malodorous blood and pus squeezed out of the cavity on the right side of his face as he spoke.

"I'm sorry." Ali raised his shaking hands from where he sat on the floor. The Australian's face was white with fear, illuminated by the dancing yellow flames from inside the hut. "I didn't know. I didn't know you were here."

Hector couldn't even move. It was as though he was floating out of his body, watching from above as the nightmare unfolded.

"What company you with, boy? Wasn't meant to be any of ours so far north," the sergeant said, then lowered his gaze across Ali's body. "And what the fuck ya'll wearing?" His lips curled in distaste.

Rickard pulled the USMC knife up from where it was lodged in the ground at the doorway of the hut. He wiped the blade down on his shirt and tucked it into his belt, taking a step out towards Ali.

"Company? I-I…"

"Company? Unit? Squad?"

"I'm, err, Australian."

"Australian?! On your feet. Hands on the wall there." Rickard narrowed his gaze, as best he could with one eye, and waved Ali over towards the hut with the barrel of his huge revolver.

Without question, Ali obeyed. As he rose to his feet, he glanced over his shoulder, probably hoping for backup. *They haven't seen me,* Hector realised, wondering how badly a hole in his face may have affected the sergeant's eyesight.

This is your chance. Hector tried to move, but it was like his feet were cemented to the ground.

Finally, Hector managed to will his body from paralysis, and started for the gun, just five or six steps away. Then, in a moment of panic, he lost all courage and darted back into cover.

What is my plan here? He was no soldier, he couldn't shoot them in the back, could he? Whatever they were. *But they killed Ricky, now they're going to kill Ali too.*

As Hector fought panic and indecision, the moment of opportunity passed.

Rickard spun his head around to the interpreter. Gaunt, colourless skin stretched too tight over the young man's bones, like clingfilm covering the carcass of a roast chicken. He must have been no older than nineteen.

"Watts, check the weapon." Rickard nodded at the gun Ali had dropped near the treeline. Hector melted back into the shadows, relieved he'd made the right choice.

The young soldier glanced nervously at Higgs, who shrugged in response. Watts then slowly stepped forward, pushing his M16 up over one shoulder.

At the rear of the group, Higgs lit up a cigarette, smoke seeping from the shrapnel wounds across his chest and throat. Neither he nor the others seemed to even be aware of their grievous conditions.

Watts reached for the pistol with spindly fingers that looked out of place even holding a gun. He passed it grip-first towards his commander. "*Kiểu Năm Tư– Type 54* copy, sir."

Rickard holstered his revolver and took the pistol. He ran his eye over it, then spat a wad of blood-filled phlegm on the ground by his boots.

"Now what in the name of Sweet Baby Jesus is an Aussie doing behind enemy lines with a gook gun?"

"It's not mine," Ali said. "I swear! I found it in a box. We were looking for this dead guy, and we dug it up with a load of gold."

Rickard slipped out the cartridge, counting the shots and smoothly reloaded it. He laughed. Higgs laughed too, black gunk and smoke leaking from the holes in his chest, as he did. Ali joined in also, the confusion and relief playing out across his face.

"Put that fuckin' thing out," Rickard suddenly exploded over his soldier. Higgs quickly dropped his smouldering cigarette and rubbed it into the ground with a guilty look on his face, like a kid whose parents had just caught him having his first cigarette.

"Next time you eat the damn pack," the sergeant growled and flicked his attention back to Ali. "This gun is a piece of shit. You know that, right?"

He nodded, keeping his eyes on the wall.

Rickard raised the pistol with his left hand, pointing it at Ali's back.

The hideous realisation of what was about to happen hit Hector like a brick and he yelped in shock.

Rickard swung towards the sound, squeezing the trigger three times in quick succession, aiming to put two into the bushes where he'd heard the voice, and then the final shot into the base of Ali's skull.

The decades-old pistol did nothing.

In a single smooth motion, Rickard's right hand slid down to his waist, drew his own revolver, and levelled it at Hector's face; his thumb pulling back the hammer.

In the moment of distraction, Em bolted out of the hut, ducking directly under Truman's arms, who, weighed down by his heavy weapon, was too slow to stop her.

The corporal took aim as Em fled into the pitch-black forest but held out for an order. He looked confident that his beast of a gun would have no problem shredding both the trees and the girl from a distance.

"Let her run," Rickard said, still aiming at Hector. "Swapping out a dumb little girl who wants to play army for a couple of traitors is a good enough deal. Besides, she ain't exactly gonna have it easy stuck on this island with no fuckin' teeth." He dropped Ali's gun into the dirt. "Now, that's what happens when you get yourself a Chinese sidearm."

While Rickard laughed, Higgs moved in behind Hector and nudged him towards the hut with the barrel of his M16.

Hector kind of wanted to shove the fact into Rickard's face that his own American-built M16s were considered one of the greatest failures in military history. However, he bit his lip. This was definitely not the situation to be a smartass.

"Took your fucking time again," Ali hissed as they were both shoved face-first against the rough wooden panels.

"Sorry."

Icy hands crunched and ground as they fastened the two prisoners' arms behind their backs. The wiry paracord bit into Hector's flesh as his wrists were bound, then tied on to Ali's front, locking them together like an old-style chain gang.

"Now…" Rickard grinned. "I got a few questions for you, boys, and I expect answers."

Hector shuddered.

"But first, I gotta take a shit. Truman, bag 'em."

Everything went dark.

Chapter Eighteen

Day One
23:34
Present Day

From the first day Anna had met her, Em had been getting them both into trouble. Something about bad situations seemed to draw the aspiring model like a moth to a flame.

One night in particular stood out among the many. She and Em had been getting along well with a trio of guys, ones who seemed different from the usual type they met out on the town, classier and more worldly.

They had a booth reserved in one of the capital's biggest clubs, an underground techno dance hall with an all-chrome interior and headache-inducingly loud music.

From where Anna sat on a sticky, red leather sofa with a glass of Royal Salute Twenty-One in her hand, the strobe-lit dance floor seemed like an endless sea of writhing, glamorous bodies. She couldn't shake the feeling that this was Em's world, or the one she so badly aspired to become a part of at least, not hers.

At the time, the capital's nightlife had seemed a million miles away from the grotty little apartment Anna shared with her parents, two sisters, and grandmother, even though it was only a five-minute trip on the back of Em's Vespa.

The promises of elegance and illusions of wealth were probably what had attracted Anna to the take the job working for a fashion magazine in the first place. She cared little about the clothes themselves, and certainly didn't have thousands of dollars to blow at downtown boutique stores like most of the people in the club seemed to. Still, it was an exciting scene to be part of, for a few hours a week at least. Anna could certainly understand the attraction for Em.

One of the better-looking men in the group, a typical hipster guy with swept-over hair and a goatee, squeezed in next to Anna and waved at the bartender for another bottle, this time Grey Goose Vodka, pulling out a wad of cash that was probably more than her family had to spare in a year.

On the other side, Em, in a low cut, silver cocktail dress that seemed to always attract a certain type, giggled and rubbed up against another member of the trio.

The guy — Anna thought he said his name was Dat, but it was hard to hear over the pounding techno beat — filled up a third of her glass, and the group toasted, the men shouting to finish the drinks in one, as was customary.

Anna tried her best, not wanting to look gauche among the sophisticated clubgoers, but found it hard to stomach much of the strong liquor.

After a few minutes, she had started to feel a little lightheaded and spacey. She put that down to the booze and balloons of laughing gas they'd been passing around all night, coupled with the fact that Em had persuaded her to go out without her glasses on.

"Don't worry. It'll pass," Em told her when she voiced her concerns. "You need to relax and cut loose sometimes."

As the feeling of disconnect swelled, Anna knew she should be scared, but more than anything, she was tired. Her eyelids were so heavy it was almost impossible to keep them open.

She let her eyes rest for just a moment and woke up with a jolt, suddenly somewhere completely different. The new room had dim lighting and smelt like old ashtrays and cheap perfume. The *thud-thud* of techno still pounded, not far away but muffled and distant.

Warm hands, sticky from spilled liquor, were climbing up beneath her dress and rubbing at her crotch. Anna tried to shout but didn't have the energy.

It was like the kind of dream where you needed to run, but your body refused to respond, or it felt as though you were trying to jog through a knee-deep pool of sticky honey.

A sudden thunderous smash shocked Anna back to her senses. She was half-dressed, lying on a sticky red sofa with broken glass littering the floor around her. The disgusting, sticky-fingered man she could now see had been Dat was lying on his side with a massive gash on his head. Em was standing over them, the remains of the shattered bottle of Grey Goose still in her hand.

"We have to go," Em said, her voice sounding distant and distorted. Her pupils were as wide as saucers, the result of some unknown cocktail of pills, but there was definite fear in there too.

Eventually, with an arm around her neck, Anna's friend half-carried and half-dragged her across the dance floor. The glitz and glamour were all but gone. Now it seemed more like the club was filled with sparkling zombies, writhing in pain to the beat of terrible electronic music. In that moment of half-hallucinated cognisance, Anna could have sworn she was seeing the dancers' true, ugly natures for what they really were.

To their rear, the other pair of men who had been with them in the booth were pushing through the clubbers, trying to catch up. Seconds before they made it, Anna and Em fell through the double doors out into the calm predawn air.

When their pursuers stumbled out a few moments later, the dishevelled women were already being helped to their feet. A pair of traffic police officers, both armed with tasers and pistols, happened to have pulled up outside the club. Dat's accomplices took one look and slipped quietly back inside. The two young women weren't worth the trouble.

From that day, Anna had known that despite her vices and mistakes, Em would always have her back. Now, she intended to make sure that the feeling was mutual.

Anna awoke after dozing up against a tree for an hour or so. She had Hoa's head cradled on her lap while the old woman slept. They hadn't so much as moved an inch since Hector and Ali left, despite being just ten feet away from Ricky's corpse.

As the darkest part of the night came and went, Anna finally admitted the horrible truth that she'd been trying not to believe. Neither Hector, Ali, nor Em were coming back.

She cursed herself for being such a fool yet again. She and Hoa were the two weakest members of the group by far. It was a mistake to let the others go off, leaving them alone. Staring down at Ricky's body, the fear and guilt of her impassivity grew too much to handle. *You have to find Em. She'd do the same for you.*

"We need to go," Anna said, shaking Hoa lightly by the shoulder. The pair of them had barely spoken since coming across Ricky's body. In fact, the old woman had said very little since they finished the dig for her brother.

Hoa seemed dazed and confused as she pulled herself up to a sitting position. Then finally, a look of sad recollection crawled its way across the old woman's face as the events of the past twenty-four hours rose to the surface. "I don't remember the way back," Hoa mumbled. "I'm sorry. This has been a hard day."

"It's okay. I think I know it. But we shouldn't use the torch unless we have to. We don't want to attract any more attention than absolutely necessary."

"Yes," Hoa said. "The darkness doesn't bother me."

Of course not. Anna knew the village the old woman came from. Although just two hours from the capital city, it was right up in the mountains where they'd only had electricity for the last ten or fifteen years.

The sky was hazy and grey by the time Anna and Hoa reached the camp. An ominous predawn mist was already oozing over the distant mountaintops, like condensed milk pouring down into a coffee cup.

From a hundred yards out, Anna could tell something was drastically wrong. The tents were completely gone, the site was smouldering, tiny plumes of smoking embers floating up in the blue-grey air.

"Stay here," she said, resting a hand on Hoa's back, which was damp with cold sweat. Anna crept forward slowly. *Who set the camp on fire? Where is everyone?*

Forcing the fear from her exhausted mind, she took a deep breath and pushed between a pair of low-hanging branches. As Anna stepped through, a root snagged her foot and she tumbled face-first into the clearing at the side of the hut. Between the darkness and the surprise of the fall, it took a moment for her to even notice the gun that lay a few inches from her nose. It was the weapon from the box. *How the heck did that get here?*

She snatched it up and clambered to her feet, checking around the camp, peering at the shadows to make sure she wasn't being watched. After almost a minute of hearing nothing but the buzz of cicadas, and seeing nothing but forest, Anna decided they were alone and called Hoa out.

The old woman tottered forward, a look of despair on her face. "This is our fault. We disturbed the dead, the hungry souls that can't find peace."

Anna gave her an agreeing smile, which was all she could manage right now. She beckoned Hoa towards the hut and kicked away some of the broken glass from the floor, trying not to focus on what looked like fresh blood and shards of teeth. A few embers were still burning in the centre of the structure, so she pushed one log back over onto the coals with her foot and it started to smoulder.

"Well, what can we do about it?" All of Anna's confidence, along with any intentions of going after Em, Hector, and Ali, drained quickly. She was a weak little girl from a poor family. What could she possibly hope to achieve?

"We have to help them. The innocent people who suffered here. It's the only way any of us will be allowed to leave."

Anna chewed her lip, feeling the weight of the cold steel in her hands. In her dehydrated, sleep deprived brain, Hoa's words almost made sense.

"I'm going to find some water. You get some rest, then in a couple of hours, you can keep watch and I'll sleep."

The old woman nodded and slowly lowered herself down until she was lying on the floor in a foetal position, with her head on one arm.

Anna crept out of the hut. She found some bottled water and the remains of their lunch—a couple of leftover tubes of sticky rice—scattered at the side of the building. She scooped as much as she could into her arms, keeping the ancient weapon ready in one hand, her heart pounding all the while.

Not wanting to make a second trip outside, Anna left the supplies near the doorway and edged a few feet into the trees and squatted down. It wasn't until after they'd returned to camp that the hunger, pain in her feet, and the desperation to piss returned, as though her body was now adjusting to the trauma of the night.

After finishing up, Anna slipped back inside. Hoa was shivering as she slept, looking restless, occasionally shaking and twitching as though plagued by an uncomfortable dream, no doubt reliving some horrific past event.

Slumping up against the wall opposite the entrance, Anna pointed the gun towards the door, the only way in. She was determined not to let herself fall asleep. Not to let her guard down again.

Chapter Nineteen

Day Two
05:44
Present Day

Warmth radiated down from the tin roof. Shafts of sunlight pierced through the holes, crept across the floor, and climbed up onto Anna's face. For a moment, her exhausted mind thought she was back at home with the sun peering in through the honeycombed concrete walls of her old apartment building.

Before Anna could recall where she was or why, an icy, calloused hand clamped over her mouth. She fought to breathe but could barely get a taste of air past the strength of her attacker's grip. In panic, she bit down hard into the flesh and her mouth filled with thick, oil-like blood that tasted distinctly of death.

"Shh," the voice whispered, as if her teeth sinking deep into his hand meant nothing.

Anna thrashed and kicked, but the shadowy figure towering over her was strong, too strong. There was no doubt in her mind that he could have killed her at any moment. But he hadn't. Not so far, anyway.

Anna went limp, figuring it would be better to save her energy.

The hold released and she skidded away from her attacker, out of the shadows and towards the door. As her hands and knees scraped through the mud, glass, and ash that littered the floor, she realised Hoa was now gone.

Anna clambered up on shaking legs until she was facing the shadowy figure. "Where is sh—"

He stepped forward into the light and her voice cut off. Anna's mouth silently clapped up and down, like a carp trying to snatch flies from the air.

The man, if you could call him that, wore an archaic army uniform and had a Russian rifle strung with a braided green cord across his back. His hair was in a short and neat military cut, but it was his colour that really shook her. He was dark-skinned but eerily washed out, like an old sepia-style photograph, and his eyes were so bloodshot they were almost entirely red.

Anna's attention then fell to the soldier's wounds. Three fat bullet holes ran across his chest from hip to shoulder as though he was wearing a perforated sash made of lead. The worst of them, however, was a long gash that ran across his throat like a twisted smile. The skin curled back on the top and bottom as though it were a pair of lips. Cream-coloured tendons beneath had split like overstretched elastic, adding the illusion of a set of teeth to the nightmarish maw.

Anna's heartbeat thundered in her ears, and her legs turned to jelly. The wooden wall cracked as her head bounced off it on her way to the ground.

"Are you alright?" a voice murmured softly in her mother tongue. Anna opened her eyes, and her mind kicked back into action. She gasped for air, too terrified even to scream, and gripped her eyes shut again. *This has to be a bad dream.*

Anna couldn't say how long passed before she finally gave in to the urge to look at the demonic figure, still sensing his presence before her. *It's not a dream.* She whispered a prayer. First to God and then to the Buddha, hoping one of them was listening.

"It's okay," he whispered in a calm, even friendly tone.

Despite his mortal injuries, the soldier seemed strangely normal in how he acted. He was about her age, or maybe a little older, although it was hard to tell. He had a firm jaw and a flat, slightly crooked nose that added asymmetry and might have even made him handsome if he wasn't, literally, a walking corpse.

Behind him stood a larger man, dressed in a similar uniform, a scoped rifle slung across his back. The second soldier's head had a slanted hole through it, set at about forty-five degrees from above the temple to just beneath his cheekbone. From the big man's side-on position, Anna could see daylight through his skull. A fist-sized chunk of his left thigh was missing—probably the result of a gunshot— which should have made standing, let alone walking, impossible.

Two of the fingers on his right hand were twisted horribly, at a ninety-degree angle, but still somehow appeared to function. Apparently, the physics of their injuries meant little to these men.

"I need you to keep calm," the first man with the smiling throat said, his vocal cords shaking in the gap as he spoke.

This is impossible, Anna told herself.

"Can you do that?" The soldier's accent was strange, kind of classic sounding, like the actors in the black and white movies she'd watched with her parents as a child.

Anna swallowed and gave him a nod, her lips pursed so tight together she thought they might never open again.

"What are you doing here?" he asked.

"I... I'm looking for my friend. I need to find her."

"Why are you speaking like that?" the big man at the rear asked. His thick eyebrows furrowing as if caterpillars were sitting across his square face.

"Your friend. She one of us or one of *them*?" the man at the front questioned, his reaction less extreme, but his eyes suspicious.

"She's like me," Anna answered, desperately trying to avoid referring to herself and the deceased soldiers with the same pronoun.

"No one comes or goes without us knowing," the man behind said. He rested a hand on his comrade's shoulder and spoke quietly. "I don't like this, sir. What are the chances they'd show up at the same time?"

"It could be coincidence," the leader answered in a hushed tone.

"Bullshit. She's obviously one of their whores. Look at her! Put a bullet in her head before it's too late."

"I'm not," Anna begged. "I swear, I'm one of you."

"No, Long. That'd make us no better than them. We take the girl with us. This way, we either save a life or have a hostage."

"A hostage?" Anna said, her face twisted in disbelief. "What exactly do you think is going on here?"

The leader stared right into her eyes and placed a cold hand on her shoulder, as if he was breaking a piece of bad news. "The same thing that's been happening for as long as any of us can remember ma'am… War."

Anna was still trying to wrap her head around what she was seeing and hearing when Hoa appeared at the edge of the tree line. Her face was lily white, her mouth ajar, her jaw trembling as she stepped into the clearing.

The leader spun on the spot, pulling the Kalashnikov from his back, taking aim at the old woman and then froze too.

Long, a few steps behind him, did the same, waiting for an order. "Sir?"

"Truong?" Tears were streaming down Hoa's wrinkled cheeks. The dead man looked almost as stunned as she was.

"Mother?!" he asked, his eyebrows raised in disbelief. "What are you doi—"

"No." A smile broke through her tears. She was laughing. "It's me… Hoa."

A faraway look in the dead man's eyes gave some insight into the crushing confusion he must have felt. "Hoa," she said again, this time with more insistence. "You used to call me *Hoa Xíu Xíu—Tiny Flower*. I knew I'd find you. I just knew it."

The soldier reached out and rested his palm on her cheek, a glimmer of recognition in his eyes. "Little Hoa? But you're so... so old."

"My dear brother," she said after a moment's silence, "what ever have they done to you?"

"Me? I'm fine." Truong ran his hands across his cold, pale face, not seeming to even be aware of the gaping hole in his throat. Hoa averted her gaze as though she were feeling the pain in his place.

"How long has it been?" Truong asked, his hand still on her face. "I can't quite remember."

Half laughing and half crying, Hoa wrapped her arms around the dead man's bloodied torso, placing her head on his shoulder. "It's been a lifetime."

Truong held her tight.

"I've missed you," she said. "More than anything."

"I've missed you too, *Hoa Xíu Xíu*."

Anna couldn't believe what she was seeing. Such a mix of joy, sorrow, and sickness was something she couldn't even comprehend.

While Long's and Anna's focus was entirely upon the reunion before them, the bizarre assembly failed to notice the team surrounding them.

The first man came storming from the trees like a wild animal, crashing the butt of his weapon into the back of Truong's head with a vicious thud. The young soldier's legs crumpled, and he fell forward onto Hoa, pinning the old woman down on the ground beneath him.

Just as Long raised his gun, an explosion ripped through the forest. A bullet thundered into the back of the big man's thigh, throwing a mush of dried blood forward as it exited from the front, slotting perfectly through the previous wound in his leg.

Long went down, just in time for the dark-haired American who had hit Truong to step on his hand with a heavy boot and prise the rifle from his fingers, re-breaking two of them in the process with a disgusting crunch.

In the melee, Anna tried to flee but lost her footing and soon found a knee on the back of her neck. Needles were stabbing her throat as the enemy soldier forced her face down into the mixture of ash and mud.

To her left, Hoa slithered free from under her brother and scrambled for what remained of the tents. She grabbed the only thing within range, Ricky's bag, and pulled off one of the fold-up spades.

A shorter man with blonde hair and half a face paced over to the old woman as she clambered to her feet. Hoa was brandishing the spade like a club, aiming the lethal sharpened edge towards him.

The soldier sighed, as if the whole situation was exasperating. "Put the damn shovel down right now and maybe I'll let you live."

"YOU KILLED MY BROTHER... AGAIN!" Hoa screamed at him in Vietnamese, her face contorted with rage and sadness. It didn't matter that he didn't speak her language. She was hysterical.

The soldier whipped an American cowboy-style gun from a holster on his waistband with a flourish and trained the barrel on her. "Last chance to play along."

"Please. Do what he says," Anna shouted, struggling to get the words out with a knee across the back of her neck.

Hoa nodded slowly, as if coming to her senses, realising that there was no way she could win this fight. *Thank God.*

The old woman bent forwards to put the tool down on the ground and the soldier took a step towards her. At the last moment Hoa suddenly swung upwards with the spade, her whole-body weight thrown behind the attack aimed at the American's throat.

Its razor-sharp cutting edge skimmed the soldier's torso and practically shaved his face as he leaned back, a hair's width out of range.

The weapon completed its upward journey and continued over Hoa's shoulder, spinning her around with its momentum. She landed feebly on the ground, facing away from her attacker. The old woman's gaze met Anna's. Her eyes were spitting fire.

"Stupid old bitch," the half-faced soldier growled and stamped a heavy boot down on her back.

Hoa spat a string of furious curses at the American. He smiled and twirled the revolver in his hand until he was brandishing it like a club.

"NO!" Anna screamed as he raised the weapon high and brought it down with brutal force on the back of Hoa's head, caving the rear of her skull in like a collapsing souffle.

The old woman, who had wanted nothing more than to end her brother's suffering, looked stunned for an instant before her chin dropped down in the mud. Hoa's eyes rolled back into her head as a thick, warm stream of blood matted with her white hair.

Chapter Twenty

Day Two

05:53

Fifty Years Ago

After trekking two miles west and circling around the upper ridge of the mountain in darkness, Sang had reached unfamiliar ground and therein faced a dilemma. To continue on blindly, hoping she was moving in the right direction, or to rest until daybreak and reassess. Only after asking herself what her husband would do, had she made a decision.

The morning light revealed that Sang had made the correct choice. She'd stopped less than twenty yards from a sharp bank, which would have given her a quick trip to the valley floor had she tried to push on.

From her current vantage point, Sang could see the entire south-western side of the lake, dotted with distant spires of stone. Before the waters, patches of steam rose from the treetops, catching rays of sunshine as they climbed towards the heavens. She wished she could take a minute to watch the sun rise fully, but daylight had also brought her another important discovery.

Truong and Long's tracks were subtle, just the odd broken branch or sandal-shaped print that had landed in soft mud. But it gave Sang confirmation of their route and knowing she was at least going in the right direction was invigorating.

When the trail petered out another hour later, however, it felt like Sang was back to square one.

"Where did you go?" she shouted in frustration and kicked a tree almost hard enough to break her toes, immediately regretting it.

After a few minutes of wallowing in self-pity, Sang decided that moaning was going to do nothing to protect Truong, Long, Ly, or any of the other people she cared for. *You wanted to be a soldier*, she thought. *Think like a soldier then.*

Sang combed the area until she found what she was looking for. She pulled off her sweaty, dark-green jacket and reached one side of it around the trunk of a tall but spindly jackfruit tree.

She made a loop for each hand, then leaning backwards, with the material taking the slack and her rubber-soled shoes gripping well, she walked up the trunk. Sang was soon ten feet above the hilltop canopy, which was probably a hundred feet more above the valley proper.

Sitting among the huge, spiky fruits that grew from each limb and emitted a sweet but pungent aroma, made her stomach growl.

Sang pushed the thoughts of food from her mind for the time being and scanned the valley to the west for any sign of movement. Save for the odd monkey rustling the branches, or a flicker of colour as a songbird took flight, there was nothing. She hung back, putting her weight into the material and waited, her father's voice echoing in her head. *Patience is a virtue.*

Sang thought back to her father, her mother, and her little brother. Were they safe? Were they still at home or had they fled for the countryside like most of the other families that had the means or opportunity to do so?

Almost twenty-two months had passed since Sang had seen their faces. Even though the few years that preceded her leaving had been nothing short of awful, she now missed them terribly.

The day she received the letter from her childhood sweetheart was one that had changed her life forever. When the mysterious envelope had arrived, she was shocked to learn that not only was Truong still alive, but that he was now an officer. He had written modestly, explaining how he'd been promoted for acts of valour and removed from frontline duty to command a strategic and relatively safe outpost along the supply trail.

That night, she had packed a bag, taking only a few clothes, food, and photographs of her family from before the war had torn them apart. She'd been a coward, taking the easy way out by leaving a note that explained why she had to go.

The first time Sang had even brought up the idea of joining Truong when he signed up for the army, her father had beaten her harshly, and made her swear in front of the ancestral altar that she would never do it. She hadn't even mentioned their intention to marry, knowing she'd be guilted out of it with claims that she was "above his station" and that it would bring shame to her family.

The young woman had waited for the wail of air raid klaxons to sound that evening, aware that everyone except for thieves or soldiers would be in a shelter. She then slipped out of her window, clambered over the rooftop and down onto the pitch-black streets below, her mind a maelstrom of fear, excitement, and anticipation for who and what she might find in the south.

A rustle of branches somewhere close by snapped Sang back to here and now. Had she imagined it? *No.*

The sound of another stick breaking underfoot confirmed her suspicions. Someone was close by.

Sang shimmied down the tree, slipped back into her jacket, slung Ares over her shoulder. She then skidded down the hillside, catching a thick layer of sticky mud between her toes.

On the valley floor, it took her only a few minutes to locate a trail of broken branches. Although the Americans moved fast and kept their voices low, they were heavy-footed and left a clear path for her to follow. They were certainly not as at home in the jungle as her people.

Staying just far enough behind that she was out of view, Sang followed the squad for the next two hours, listening for any sign of Truong or Long. *They must be tracking the Americans too or still searching for a spoor*, she figured. Any other options she couldn't bear thinking about. Either way, she needed to keep following.

The squad weaved through the valley, no doubt searching for a pathway up the mountain. Eventually, they came to a river that cut through the heart of the island and created a natural break in the trees. It flowed out from beneath the hillside, meaning that the soldiers would need to cross it at some point if they hoped to keep heading south.

As the squad approached the water's edge, they stopped, probably pausing to drink and refill their canteens. Sang smiled to herself, knowing full well how much bat excrement ended up in that water.

Instead of coming any closer behind them and risking being exposed, Sang split off to their right and came back to the river further upstream.

Reaching the bank, she stowed Ares across her back and lay down on her stomach amongst the tall goosegrass that burst out from the shore like clumps of unruly hair.

Trying to ignore the huge spiders she sent scurrying and the hairy, yellow and grey caterpillars that called the foliage home, Sang crawled forward.

She rounded a bend in the river and almost shouted in surprise as she came across a soldier, twenty yards ahead, kneeling by the stream and filling up his canteen.

The young man cleaned his face, rubbed the dirt and sweat from his spectacles, and swilled the water round his mouth. He certainly didn't look evil, not like the GIs she'd seen in the propaganda posters stuck up across Hanoi. In fact, he looked more like a bookish student than someone who raped women and bayonetted children. Then she remembered that fateful night and the taste of Kien's blood on her lips. *No. That's what they want us to think.*

A dozen yards further on, a second soldier with the darkest skin she had ever seen was crouched down over a plastic covered map that was spread out on the leaves.

To his right stood a heavy-set figure with short, blonde hair and thick stubble—a sergeant. He stood proud and strong, with his hands on his hips, exuding an air of dangerous confidence. His eyes were wide and fierce, as if he could explode at any moment like one of the cheap Chinese grenades they had stockpiled in the cavern.

The leader's brow furrowed as he listened to the squatting soldier. *If they're already lost, that can only be good a thing, can't it?*

"Watts," he called out suddenly, making Sang jump. Thankfully, no one seemed to notice the slight rustle in the goosegrass. "Get over here."

"Yes, sir." The young man at the riverside stowed his canteen and ran off. Sang slid slowly down alongside the stream, sticking to the rushes, and right then, her worst nightmare came into view. Truong and Long were sitting on their knees twenty feet behind the sergeant.

A third soldier, this one with a hooked nose and dark, thick eyebrows, wearing the insignia of a corporal on his arm, stood over her husband, bearing an M60 light machine gun. It was a weapon that Sang had heard the Americans referred to as "The Pig" because of its sheer size and greed for ammunition. Despite the stifling humidity, the sight of the massive weapon sent a shiver down her spine.

Truong's expression was grim, his face was bloodied and bruised, his features now distorted beneath cuts and swellings. An all-out rage burned in the pit of Sang's stomach.

While the sergeant spoke to two members of the squad, the black man wandered over toward the river. Out of sight, he crouched down and sneakily lit a cigarette, tucking the lighter in a pocket over his left breast. He puffed away for a minute, quickly blowing out plumes of blue-grey smoke that made Sang think of watching the boats from the roof of her childhood house as they chugged up and down the Red River.

"Higgs," the sergeant called, "you better not be doing what it smells like."

"Shit," the soldier hissed, quickly flicking his cigarette into the brush beside Sang. Flames flickered in the undergrowth for a moment until, thankfully, the damp foliage put an end to the threat.

Rickard stomped over and stared down his subordinate, making Higgs cower back despite standing a good six inches taller than his leader.

"Sorry, sir. It won't happen again."

"You're damn right it won't."

"Come on. Can't be that bad."

Rickard gritted his teeth. "I know twelve dead men who would disagree."

Higgs stared down at his feet for a moment, as if having suddenly realised why he was wrong. "What happened, sir?"

Rickard cleared his throat. "Back on my first tour, we were travelling through this nasty little valley— thick jungle, humid as hell—not too different from this one. It was meant to be unoccupied, but the gooks had followed us, watching the trail of smoke like a goddamn neon sign hanging over our heads.

"When we finally got to the end of the valley, they were waiting on three sides. They came down on my squad like a fucking hammer.

"I took a bullet in the shoulder from a sniper and hit the ground. Somehow, in the middle of the slaughter, I was able to crawl free. I made it to a river, and while my squad was screaming and dying behind me, I dropped into the water and let the current take me."

"Jesus."

"That wasn't the end of it either. I got washed up downstream at this little village that night. A local girl found me half-dead and took me back to her family. They hid me while I recovered. They hated the fucking North almost as much as us."

Rickard spat at his feet in disgust.

"It didn't take long for word to spread, though. The Reds came soon enough. They killed the girl and her parents, and I spent the next two weeks walking on a rope behind the northerners, like a fucking dog. No doubt they figured they'd take me in and torture some information out of me."

Rickard sighed, as if bored with retelling the same story.

"How did you escape?"

"One night, my guard was the only one still awake. He wasn't a bad guy, not compared to the others, at least. So, I waved him over, asking for a smoke."

"And?"

"He laughed and pulled out a couple, putting one between my lips and one in his own. They'd tied my hands in front of me, so I made a show of struggling to light up. When he leaned in to help, I pulled the machete from his belt with both hands and jammed it up under his chin before he could even shout."

"What about the others?"

"The northerners are wily fuckers. They all spread out at night and string up hammocks in the trees, so if they get bombed, the whole squad doesn't get taken out in one. All I had to do was work my way down the line. A rucksack over the face and a machete across the throat makes a man real quiet, real quick."

Rickard mimed the cutting action. There was a grim smile on his face, but his eyes seemed to tell a different story altogether. Even *he* couldn't have enjoyed that much killing.

"I grabbed as much of their supplies as I could carry and hiked south for another week. When I finally found our boys, it was back in the same damn valley. They sent me down to Saigon for debriefing soon after. You know what they gave me for running away? Leaving my squad to die and hiding in some shitty little village?"

"No, sir."

"A fucking medal. That day, I vowed never to make the same mistake again. I'd already lost everyone that mattered to me. All I could do then was promise to keep fighting and make sure I always kept my men alive."

Higgs stared in silence.

"Now," Rickard barked as though suddenly snapping back to the here and now. "Give me the damn pack."

Higgs slid the smokes from his pocket and held them out solemnly towards Rickard.

"Eat," the sergeant said.

"What? I—"

"You heard me. Eat the fucking pack right now. Or I'll have you stripped and court martialled for disobeying a direct order."

Higgs glanced at his unit for support. Truman shrugged with a half-smile as if to say "I told you so" while Watts stared at his own feet.

What in the hell is wrong with him? Sang wondered, as the black soldier slowly raised a cigarette to his lips and began to chew, retching and choking as he tried to force one after another down his throat.

Three smokes down, the sergeant seemed satisfied. He turned and chatted in a low volume with Watts for two or three minutes, then waved the corporal over. Higgs finished washing out his mouth in the stream, and hobbled back towards the map, about as pale as it was possible for him to look.

"Alright. Let's try this again, shall we, boys?" Rickard said, hovering over Truong.

Watts translated the orders, speaking almost perfect Vietnamese. Sang didn't know if she was more surprised at his skill, or that the Americans had even gone to the trouble of bothering to ask questions. Normally, they would just drop napalm and burn the skin off her people's backs or bomb their towns into oblivion.

This was no normal squad, she realised. They were some kind of special undercover unit sent behind enemy lines to kill, sabotage, and destroy, starting with the man she loved.

Sang set her jaw and pulled Ares softly to her chest. She rolled onto her front, biting her lip to stop it from shaking, and took aim at Rickard's head.

Chapter Twenty-One

Day Two
07:15
Fifty Years Ago

Sang's hands clasped so tight around the stock of the Kalashnikov that her knuckles were white. She struggled to control her frantic breathing, mortified that she would either shoot too early and give herself away, or leave it too late.

Corporal Truman, the oldest man in the team, with the wiry build and dark hair, approached the captives with obvious intent. He swung his lanky arm, smacking Long across the face with an audible slap, and split his lip. It was the type of blow designed to soften a prisoner up rather than do any real damage.

Truong would never talk. He had too much on the line. However, she couldn't be as sure about Long. Without any children or a wife to protect, his only restraint would be his honour, and how long that could survive in the face of torture was anyone's guess.

Unless she did something, they would both die soon, regardless. *You are a soldier*, Sang ordered herself. *Today you must prove it.*

Only as she flicked up the safety catch on Ares did Sang realise how badly her hands were shaking. The bolt of her weapon was clinking softly as she broke from Rickard to track the corporal's movement instead.

She'd fired the gun plenty in training but turning it on another human being was a different matter altogether. *Do I even have what it takes to kill a man in cold blood?*

A moment later, Truman turned his attention to Truong, kicking him in the chest with his steel-capped boot, showing that the Americans' footwear was good for something else other than giving them skin infections in the hot, damp jungle. Seeing Truong hit the floor, winded and struggling to breathe through the pain, Sang had her answer, and it was definitive. *Yes, I do.*

Watts continued to deliver the sergeant's line of questioning, leaning over Truong, translating his words quietly. From her angle, Sang could see the fear in the young soldier's eyes. He looked almost as scared as she was.

The translator soon turned back to Rickard and muttered something to him, his eyes darting around nervously.

"Fine. Then we'll do this the hard way," Rickard said, suddenly not caring in the slightest about the volume of his voice.

Truong had been right. He was making a deliberate show of things, hoping to draw his enemies out. *Does he know I'm watching?*

The sergeant whipped a long-barrelled silver revolver from a holster at his waist and pressed the steel barrel to Long's head. "You got five seconds to point us in the right direction."

Watts translated the order.

"Five. Four."

Long was trembling but did his best to remain calm. His eyes fixed on the ground as he stoically awaited death.

He's bluffing, Sang was certain. She couldn't risk blowing her cover yet, not until the last moment. He was trying to trick them into speaking, that was all.

"Two."

She braced to fire.

"One."

Sang froze.

BOOM.

A cloud of red mist exploded from the side of Long's head, coating her husband's face. Sang bit her tongue, drawing blood, to stifle her scream. Truong lunged for the sergeant in response, trying to power his way through, but Higgs smashed him in the side of the head with a rifle butt. *He actually did it!*

Tears of guilt and anger streaming down Sang's cheeks soon shook her from the trance. Her vision fixed on Long's wide-eyed, empty stare towards the heavens.

"It's respectful of you not to sell out your brothers," Rickard continued, staring down at Truong. "If there's one thing I know in this world, it's the duty a leader feels to his men. But now it's just you. No one ever needs to know what you say here."

"FUCK YOU!" Truong spat in broken English, spraying bloody spittle across Rickard's face.

The sergeant laughed and wiped it aside with his sleeve.

"I am a man of my word. I'm a warrior, like you. Tell me what I need to know, and you'll live to fight another day. Maybe someday you can come find me, get your revenge, or die trying. That'd put a pretty little bow on things, wouldn't it?"

The sergeant spun his gun on his finger, taking aim at Sang's husband.

"Or you can die for no good reason, here and now. Your call, Kemosabe."

Truong said nothing.

"Five." Rickard pulled the hammer back. "Four."

A sudden sense of calm washed over Sang. She'd been able to hit targets from twice this range in practice. Now, however, her angle was awkward. There was sweat was in her eyes and distracting streaks of hair stuck to her face, but she knew she could make the shot if she had to. For him.

"Three."

"Two."

"WAIT!" Sang screamed. All eyes fell on the long grass at the bank of the river.

"Don't kill him. I'll talk." Sang's English wasn't as good as her French, but it might be enough to negotiate. She clambered to her feet, leaving Ares lying in the undergrowth.

The next moment happened so fast she could barely take it in.

Truong leapt up at Higgs, thrusting his forehead into the soldier's nose, shattering it like a cheap china plate. Simultaneously, he tore the rifle from Higgs' hands and twisted it towards the other soldiers. Both Rickard and Truman spun from Sang to face their escaping captive while Watts simply locked up with fear.

Before Truong could take aim, the corporal unleashed a burst from 'The Pig'. The first four shots thudded into the ground, but another three landed in her husband's chest. The impact taking him clean off his feet. *NO!*

As if operating on instinct alone, Sang dived for Ares and unloaded a volley of fire at anyone standing. The kickback from the weapon nearly threw it into her face, but she re-aimed and released another burst.

The sergeant hit the ground an instant before her shots landed and dragged Truong in front of his body as a human shield. Truman took at least two bullets in the face and chest, then disappeared from Sang's view into the undergrowth, his screams fast becoming a gurgle. The remaining blast disappeared among the trees.

Sang tried to get an aim on Rickard, but she could only just see him through the grass, as he lay with one arm wrapped around her husband's forehead, extending his body outwards to maximise his cover.

In what could only have been a move of pure spite, the sergeant drew an eight-inch combat knife from his belt, and staring into Sang's eyes, ran it across her husband's throat, splitting the flesh like meat in the market. Sang shrieked a jumbled mess of words, her brain barely able to process the horror of what she was seeing.

Half a second later, the remaining two soldiers returned fire. She barely heard a sound as bullets whipped past her and thundered into the ground at her side. In a blind mixture of shock, grief, anger, and adrenaline, Sang took the only option that remained. She ran.

Chapter Twenty-Two

Day Two
07:08
Present Day

A nearby bang jolted Hector awake. The sharp chemical stench of gunpowder wafted in a moment later. Nothing more than a few specks of light seeped through the burlap sack covering his pounding head. Dried blood matted his hair, sticking it to the rough-spun material. Beyond that was what he guessed to be a tree trunk. The air was thick and warm. As the taste of gunpowder faded from the back of his throat, the aroma of mould and sickly-sweet overripe fruit overtook it.

Where am I? It took a good half a minute for his concussed brain to pull memories of the night back from the edge of an abyss.

After getting captured, the soldiers had led him and Ali through the forest for nearly an hour before ordering them to kneel. Anticipating that they were about to be shot, Hector had heard Ali make a break for it and followed his lead a heartbeat later, bolting in the direction of where he thought the treeline might be. This tactic had ended abruptly with a rifle butt thundering into the side of his temple, and the world spinning as he hit the ground.

Hector's hands, fastened behind his back, were ice cold and totally numb. He tried wriggling his fingers, and only after a few minutes did the stabbing sensation of pins and needles emerge.

Rubbing the back of his head against the bark, Hector eventually worked the bag up an inch. Spurred on by the taste of fresh air, he used his tongue to push it up further and further, uncaring that the material tasted like old sweat and piss mixed with rotten meat.

Finally, with a series of quick nods, he pushed the sack up over his eyes and a glorious, green light filled his vision. Rays of warm morning sun filtered down through the canopy, catching the condensation and imbuing the forest with a mystical glow.

A hundred unanswered questions swirled about in Hector's mind. But only two of them seemed to matter right now. *Who did they just shoot? Why have they left me here?*

Scanning the area, Hector noted an inclined pathway to his left that led over a ridge towards a break in the trees. He wondered if it was a river or even the lake on the other side. Either way, it sounded like that was where his captors had stopped.

Hector pulled and twisted at the rope around his hands, trying to loosen his bindings so he could investigate. He ground the material between the bark and his wrists until they were chafed and bloody, but to no avail.

Exhausted after minimal exertion, beaten down with the stress, heat, fear, and injury, Hector slumped, his head hanging. Only in that moment of defeat did he notice a scratching coming from his rear, from the far side of the tree.

"Ali," he whispered over his shoulder, uncertain if it was friend or foe.

"Hector?" a soft voice replied.

"Anna?"

"Oh fantastic," she replied. "I thought I was alone."

"Are you okay? Are you hurt?"

"No, I'm fine. Ali is here on this side as well. He's unconscious, but still breathing."

"Oh, thank God," Hector replied. "Can you see anything?"

"Yes. I got the bag off my head a while ago."

"So, I assume you saw those *things*?"

"We did but—"

"Wait, where's Hoa?"

"We met her brother—the Vietnamese leader."

"Met? He was alive?"

"I wouldn't go that far…"

"What happened then? How did you end up here?"

"The Americans ambushed us. They killed Hoa and took the two Vietnamese soldiers as prisoners. Then, they led us here with bags over our heads and tied me up with you. The soldiers were taken off in your direction for some reason… Did you find Em?" The worry in her voice hadn't faded.

"Yes."

"Is she…?"

"No. Thank God. She ran when we interrupted them… they were about to, well, rape her."

Anna let out a slow breath, pained by the imagery. "It's like they're trapped in the past," she said. "Not even aware that they're dead. Hoa's brother thought he was still at war."

"I don't believe it," Hector said. "This must be some kind of group hallucination or something." The idea sounded so stupid now he heard it out loud. But what other explanation could there be?

"I know what I saw. It was clear as day," Anna snapped. "You literally held Ricky's wounds as he died. I watched them club Hoa's head in. She passed away a foot in front of me while I could do nothing." She took a deep breath, fighting back tears. "It's *not* a bad dream, as much as I wish it was."

"I'm sorry," Hector said. "It's just, this is a lot to take in. But I agree, there's no rational explanation for what we saw."

"It's okay."

Hector let out a weak chuckle.

"What is it?"

"I remembered what Van told us about there being more dangerous things than just the jungle out here. She certainly wasn't overstating it, was she?"

"We should've listened."

"Well, hindsight is always twenty-twenty. Regardless, we still need to get out of here as fast as possible. Can you try to wake up Ali?"

There was a thud as Anna hit him with something, probably her feet or knees. Finally, a long low groan mixed with mumbled Aussie curses responded. *Yes!*

"Ali, are you there, man?"

He groaned again. "This fucking sucks." His voice was muffled under the material.

"Are you hurt?"

"I dunno, my head is killing me... how much did I drink? Why'd I let you guys tie me up?"

"Well, you still sound like your usual self."

"Where are the others?"

"Hoa's gone," Anna said. "We can't find Em. Let's just focus on ge—"

A shout from the clearing interrupted her.

"Can either of you move?" Hector asked with a renewed sense of urgency. "If we're all tied together around the tree, we should try to stand up. Then maybe I could see what's going on."

"How would that help?"

"It probably won't," Hector said. "But I'd at least feel better knowing we've exhausted every option rather than sit here and wait to be executed."

"Executed?" Anna sounded one step away from a full-blown panic attack. It was pretty understandable, all things considered.

"No. Not executed. I was exaggerating," he lied. "But I don't think they're just gonna shake our hands and let us go, especially after what happened to the others."

"Man. I'm gonna kill those zombie motherfuckers," Ali growled, the lethargy leaving his voice as anger took its place. He rustled for a minute, rocking his head back and forth to get the sack off.

"How exactly do you plan on doing that?" Hector asked. "Those things are both already dead and clearly don't feel any pain… Their leader literally has half a face, and he doesn't even seem to notice."

"It's not that they don't feel it," Anna said. "It's like it hasn't even happened to them yet. The guy with Hoa's brother had a wound in his thigh and another one in his head. I saw him get shot in exactly the same spot on his leg earlier. I bet the gunshot we heard was the one that killed him."

"You think the only way they can die is the way someone killed them originally?" Hector wondered out loud.

"Bullshit," Ali said. "You gotta remove the head or destroy the brain, then job done. I've seen enough zombie movies to know that!"

"Either way, I think trying to get out of here should be the first priority. Let's try to stand—ready?"

On Hector's mark, they all pushed up to their feet and shimmied round to the left, putting him closer to the clearing.

From a standing position, Hector could make out a clear patch of grassland over the rise and a narrow river beyond it.

A moment after they made the switch, another explosion burst through the trees, followed by a quick volley of four or five more shots. By the time it stopped, Hector's ears were ringing so hard he could barely hear his own thoughts. *Who are they shooting at now?*

Two seconds later, his question was answered. A figure in combat attire and a dark-green pith helmet burst through the leaves, no more than ten feet from their position, and bolted up the hill to the east.

Suddenly, the soldier noticed the three strangers pinned against the tree and froze. Only then did Hector realise he was looking at a young woman.

She had large, dark eyes that were alight with fear. Her hair was bundled up inside the helmet, making it sit high on her head and revealing a long gash that ran from beneath her hairline down to her right eyebrow. A dark, rotten hole punctured her shoulder, mostly hidden beneath her baggy uniform. As Hector's eyes moved down, he noticed the open wound in her gut. Her shirt and skin alike flapped down, revealing a twisted mess of rotten organs.

A wave of disgust at the sheer brutality of it all swamped him. How many lives had been thrown away in the pointless battle for this island?

No one survived. That was what Ricky had said. The fact simply confirmed what Hector had suspected all along. Whether you took a life or lost one, war would make a monster out of you one way or another.

The young woman hissed a swear word in her native tongue, snatched a small brown package from her belt and threw it towards Anna. She then took off again in a wild sprint up the steep and thickly forested hill to their right.

Hector braced for a moment, half expecting to be blown to smithereens by a grenade, but the bang never came. Another few seconds passed before he put things together and realised that the object thrown to Anna was a folding knife.

When Hector spun his gaze back towards the opening, he could see three bodies on the ground, partially covered by leaves and branches of the bushes between them.

From the middle of the dead, Rickard clambered to his feet, his hands and chest dripping with blood. Whether it was his own or it belonged to their prisoners wasn't clear. The look on the sergeant's face, however, was even more deranged than it had been on their first encounter. His single remaining eye bulged watching the running woman disappear up the hillside. He laughed and raised a bloodstained hand to his mouth and shouted after her. "Run, little rabbit, run!"

Chapter Twenty-Three

Day Two
07:18
Fifty Years Ago

Ah crap. He's fading. Mike Watts could already see that Truman was half asphyxiated. The hole in his upper cheekbone looked like it was mostly superficial. Instead, it was the one in his chest that would soon end his life.

Watts figured if he could pack the wound tight, then there was a chance the injured soldier might live long enough to get surgery. That, at least, may leave Truman with the option of dying from an infection.

Watts didn't exactly like the guy, but that was no reason to condemn him to death. Besides, if Truman lived, maybe they'd seek medevac instead of pushing on. If so, the young interpreter might even see his home again one day. *God knows I deserve it after this.*

Watts slung the M16 across his shoulder and dropped to his knees, unclipping the individual first aid kit from the back of his belt and rifling through it.

Obsessive reading of training material was the only thing that had helped him make it through basic training at all. Watts knew exactly what to do with a clogged mortar launcher, all the types of mushrooms they could safely harvest in the jungle, the patterns and head shape of every poisonous snake they were likely to encounter. However, the most useful skill of all was knowing each and every emergency first aid technique from memory. Performing these things on paper, however, was a different kettle of fish from when you were kneeling over the body of a dying man.

With shaking hands, Watts ripped open Truman's shirt and grimaced at the at the sight that awaited him. A bullet had punctured the rib cage on the left-hand side of the corporal's chest, hitting the inferior lobe of the lung. He was making a guttural wheezing noise, while the scent of foul, burnt flesh that emanated from the wound was the stuff of nightmares.

As Watts worked to stem the blood flow, covering the bullet hole with his palm and stabilising the breathing, he found his thoughts drifting back to days before the war.

Growing up on a farm, even for an awkward kid like Watts, didn't come without its fair share of life lessons. He'd often been on hand to help as his father worked on sick and injured animals. Usually they could save the creatures, other times they would fail.

It was in those rare instances, when an animal was too far gone, that death could be a mercy.

Watts suspected that this was now the case with Truman, but he wasn't ready to give up hope, not if it could mean them all making it home alive. *Not yet.*

"Pass me your gauze."

"What? Why?" Higgs replied, still cradling his broken nose. The glare in his eyes said it all. "He's done. It's a waste."

"He's not. The lung is collapsing. If I pack it tight enough, he might survive."

Higgs sighed, fished a roll of gauze from his own medical kit with one hand, and reluctantly passed it over.

Watts took out his canteen and washed his hands quickly. There was nothing in the manuals about first cleaning lung wounds, and he certainly didn't want to fill it with fluid. So he stayed clear of the water, rolled the gauze up into a tight cylinder and set about packing it in the half inch-wide wound.

"Shit," Higgs muttered, catching sight of the sergeant. From his rear, Watts heard fast, heavy footsteps approaching.

"What the fuck do you think you're doing, boy?"

"S-sir?" Watts stuttered, trying to keep his voice from cracking.

"Goddamn it," he said, staring down at Truman without a hint of sadness on his face. "This man was my friend, my brother. You let him die with some fuckin' dignity."

"But, I—"

"Look into his eyes."

Watts followed the order and met Truman's eyes—glassy and panicked—as the older man approached death's door. It was sickening.

"You don't force him to hold on and suffer. I would expect the same from any of you. Now stand down."

Truman's chest was rising and falling in a frantic but steady rhythm. If Watts could save this one life, maybe there was still some hope for redemption. He'd never wanted to shoot or kill, to see men, women, and children alike torn apart in a hail of bullets, or hear them scream as their homes became infernos. *I just want to go home.*

Watts clenched his fists. "He's not dead yet. You have to let me try!"

The moment the words escaped Watts' lips, he knew he'd gone too far. This wasn't stealing off for a smoke, this was a downright insubordination. Rickard would no doubt make him eat his words, and he wouldn't get away with one or two like Higgs had done.

"I don't need to let you do shit!" The sergeant slammed a heel into Watts's chest, sending him sprawling back into the leaves.

The interpreter skidded off to the side, just in time to see Rickard pull out his massive Smith and Wesson Model 29 in a single fluid motion and take aim at the wounded man's heart. "I'm in charge here! Don't you forget that you little faggot."

"Please," Watts begged. "No more killing."

The corporal didn't scream or moan. He simply looked up in silence as though awaiting the relief.

BOOM. The gunshot sent birds scattering, and a cloud of blue smoke drifted skywards.

"Bury Truman," Rickard ordered.

"What about these?" Higgs wiped the blood from his face with his sleeve and nodded down at the bodies of two Vietnamese soldiers, or what was left of them at least.

"We'll leave them for the rats. Now get a move on. We can't afford to lose the rabbit's trail."

Chapter Twenty-Four

Day Two
07:21
Present Day

"We're screwed, aren't we, mate?"

"I think so." Hector stared at the crazed redneck sergeant heading their way, his sidearm drawn, and his eyehole seeping black and yellow pus.

"Not yet." There was a rustle as Anna slid round the tree towards Ali, having cut herself free with the running woman's blade.

She slipped the wooden handle of the folding knife into his hand, then skidded back round to her side and sat down.

"Ali, cut the rope, but don't move yet," she said. "When you're ready, I'll pretend to run for it so he chases me, then you can get Hector out. Sorry, Hector," she said. "You'll have to keep him busy until then."

It wasn't the worst plan he'd ever heard, but it was also far from the best.

Hector struggled against his ropes with shaking hands, unsure if he was trying to cause a distraction or just straight up run for it.

Five seconds later, the sergeant was glaring down at him. Although he wasn't tall, a couple of inches shorter than Hector himself, Rickard made up for that with width. Filling out his military fatigues with muscle, and clasping a ten-inch silver revolver, the man exuded an air of authority. This, coupled with his grey, half-destroyed face and the overpowering stench of decay, made the sergeant beyond terrifying.

The rope strained as Ali sawed at it. Despite Hector's panic, he *needed* to keep Rickard's focus on him and away from his friends.

"Now, what in God's name should I do with you?" The look in the sergeant's single eye cut through any remaining shreds of Hector's confidence like a laser.

"You could let us go."

Rickard laughed, snorting up a wad of bloody phlegm as he did and spitting it on the ground at his feet.

Worth a try.

"Now, I ain't got time for the little party we had planned, and I'm a curious little fella. So, I'll ask one more time only. Who are y'all, and why you working with the gooks?"

"We're not working with them," Hector said. "I swear it's true. We don't even speak their language!"

Rickard grunted in response, as if dismissing the idea as ridiculous.

"Fine. So, you won't mind if I put a few slugs into your whore?" He nodded in Anna's direction.

When Hector didn't answer, Rickard pulled back the hammer on his gun and took a step towards her. The rope was still moving; they needed more time.

"Wait!"

"I'm listening."

"She's... err." He felt like a fool for even saying it. "She's my girlfriend. That's why we're here. I came to find her."

Rickard laughed, a big booming chuckle. "You know how long I've been in this damn country?"

Hector had no idea where this was going, but he needed to keep the sergeant's focus on him. "No."

"Four years. Now, I've seen plenty of soldiers going off chasing some local pussy. But I ain't heard one yet call them his 'girlfriend'." Rickard smirked, shaking his head, then suddenly changed his tone to a growl. "Now, you got about three seconds to start spilling some truths or I start spilling blood."

The sergeant obviously had no idea how long he'd really been here. *How would he react if he found out?* Hector shuddered at the thought. "Okay. I—"

From the corner of his eye, there was a blur of motion as Anna bolted for the trees, shaking off the rope as she went. Rickard levelled his revolver. *He's not even going to bother chasing her. I have to do something.*

Just as the shot was about to fire, Hector kicked out as hard as he could at the sergeant's knees. Something crunched beneath his heel, and Rickard dropped to the ground, yelping in either pain, surprise or both.

"You're gonna die for that," he snarled and spun towards Hector. Half a second later, Ali slammed the folding knife down into Rickard's back, between his shoulder blade and his neck, with a sickening, squelchy sound.

The sergeant's hand released the gun automatically as his tendons reacted to the shock. He shouted through gritted teeth and, using his left hand, pulled the blade back out. He *must* have felt some semblance of pain, although it seemed faded and distant, like his memories.

Rickard whipped around, uncoiling like a snake, and slammed his left elbow into the Australian's jaw.

Ali's legs wobbled as he tried to stay upright but failed. His hands found the collar of Rickard's shirt and he dragged the dead sergeant down to the ground with him.

From the trees, Anna darted in, snatched up the knife and frantically started sawing through the rope around Hector's wrists. She freed him a few seconds later and shoved the weapon into his palm.

He sprang to his feet behind Rickard and Ali, who were rolling among the leaves, throwing punches at each other in a twisted mess of sweat, blood, and soil. Instead of leaping into action and thrusting the knife into the sergeant's back or neck as planned, Hector found himself once again paralysed with indecision. *Shit! What can I do? I can't stab someone.*

Just then, an opportunity presented itself. Rickard climbed on top and leaned forward, pushing down on Ali's windpipe with his forearm, while the Australian's arms and legs thrashed.

From the rear, Hector threw all of his strength into a massive soccer kick at the sticky, black mess where Rickard's groin should have been.

The sergeant roared in agony and spun, smashing a rock-hard fist into Hector's nose before he rolled off to the side, doubled over in pain.

Footsteps pounded the ground as the two remaining soldiers abandoned their grave digging and came sprinting from the river.

Ali rose to his feet, his face battered and swollen. Thick, metallic blood was washing down the back of Hector's throat, making him cough and splutter. He abandoned the knife and pulled himself up beside his friend, using the tree for balance. "Run!"

The Australian apparently had other plans. As Rickard pushed to his knees, Ali snatched the huge cowboy revolver from the ground and levelled it at the sergeant's head.

"Ali, no!"

"This prick needs to die again," he said, and squeezed the trigger.

The blast of the gunshot echoed through the forest, sending a thousand birds from the canopy into the skies. Kickback from the weapon was intense, and a thick cloud of blue, sulphur-smelling smoke erupted from the barrel.

Ali looked down to see how badly the large calibre round had destroyed the sergeant's head, but something was *very* wrong.

Rickard was untouched. He stared back up at Ali with one hand still on his groin, his single eye spitting fire.

Oh my god!

Ali swung towards Hector and Anna, just in time for them to see the satisfied smile on his face become replaced with pure panic. "That's not fair!" he said. "They can't g—"

BANG. BANG.

A pair of shots from the rear slammed into Ali's back, blowing a spray of blood out through the front of his chest. His face twisted in pain, his eyes wide, his mouth trying to speak but unable to produce any words.

"NO!"

Higgs aimed again.

Anna tackled Hector, dragging him down to the forest floor. The natural dip put them below the soldier's line of fire, as another three shots sailed overhead and blasted into the trees where they'd stood half a second before.

"Ali!" Hector said, trying to clamber back towards his friend.

Anna grabbed him by his shirt, swinging his face back towards her own. "He's dead, Hector. We need to run, or we will be too."

She was right.

Higgs came into view over the crest of the hill, the butt of his M16 resting against his shoulder. Twenty yards from their position, he took aim.

As Hector stared down the barrel of the American rifle, he prayed that death would be the end, and that he, Ali, Anna, or any of the others wouldn't end up like these abominations.

Chapter Twenty-Five

Day Two
07:33
Present Day

Every muscle in Hector's body clenched as Higgs squeezed the trigger. Nothing happened.

Whether it was the famous unreliability of the American-made M16 itself, or the half a century of corrosion added on top, Hector couldn't be sure. Either way, it didn't look like their luck was going to last for long.

Higgs smacked the side of the gun, hoping to free the ammunition jam. At the same moment, Rickard dived for his revolver, that was still locked within Ali's death grip.

Hector and Anna took off, sprinting blindly into the shadowy jungle. Five roaring shots followed moments later but miraculously slammed only into the surrounding trees.

For the first few minutes, Higgs was hot on their tails. But the sounds of snapping branches and the clink of his gun against the canteen at his side soon quieted. Surprisingly, they stopped altogether not long after. It was almost like Higgs couldn't deviate too far from his original course.

Another half hour passed before Hector's rush of adrenaline disappeared, with pain and exhaustion taking its place. The heat and humidity were draining, like they were hiking inside a sauna.

Thankfully, on the southern side of the island, the dense forest faded away and patches of straight, green bamboo replaced it. Had it not been for the cursed situation, Hector might have appreciated the beauty of it all. Right now, all he cared about was the fact that it allowed a breeze to creep through and made the experience a little less oppressive.

In a small clearing, Hector stopped and rested with his head in his arms against a thick of trunk of bamboo. After a minute, he slid down to the ground, feeling numb. Despite Ali's *many* questionable qualities, he was a good man. He hadn't deserved that. *No one deserved that.*

Anna sat opposite, wearing a similar look of hollow disbelief.

Eventually, Hector wiped the tears from the corners of his eyes with his thumbs. "It's all my fault," he said. "I should never have made everyone come."

"It's not your fault," Anna replied softly. "How could you have possibly known what was happening here? Besides, you did everything you could to help Ali. He chose to try and take revenge instead."

Hector cleared his throat, suddenly feeling embarrassed at his display of vulnerability. "I suppose you're right."

Anna moved over to sit at his side and squeezed his hand for reassurance. Even though they'd only known each other for two days, it felt like a lot longer. Hector owed it to her to keep himself together long enough for them to get to safety.

"I think we need to keep moving south," he said. "Ricky's friend should be there with the boat, shouldn't he?"

"What about Em? We can't leave her here with these psychotic soldiers who still think they're in the middle of a war."

"Agreed." Amid the mayhem, he'd actually forgotten about Em still being out there. "Maybe if we head south to the pickup point, she will have found her own way there. One thing is for sure though, we can't go charging off after her in the middle of this thing. We'll have to take our chances."

Anna looked intensely troubled. "I can't leave her… she wouldn't leave me."

"But we don't even know where Em is… Do you think she could have had the same idea as us? Where else would she have gone?"

"Honestly, I'm not sure. But knowing Em, I severely doubt she could even figure out which way is south."

Hector sighed, running a hand through his hair, thick with blood, sweat, and dirt. The side of his head hurt, but it was nothing compared to his nose, which was throbbing and grotesquely swollen. "What if we keep going for the boat? If it's there, we could ask the driver to wait while we search or get him to call for help?"

"We don't have a choice, do we?" Anna looked hopelessly conflicted. It was understandable not wanting to leave her friend, but they were a long way out of their depth, and she obviously knew it. "Okay. But how do *we* get there?"

Hector hadn't thought that far ahead. He raised one hand over his eyes, glanced up at the trees, and considered their predicament. "Well, the sun rises in the east and sets in the west. Is that still true in Asia or is that a European thing?"

"I'm a fashion and lifestyle magazine editor. What makes you think I'd know that?" She smiled again and for a moment, Hector managed to forget their horrific situation.

"Damn. Alright, I reckon it must be because the planet is still spinning the same direction." Hector was so thirsty and tired, he couldn't even tell if he was talking complete gibberish or if he'd suddenly pulled some profound wisdom out of the bag. "That means south must be that way." He pointed just off the axis from where the large mid-morning sun hung overhead, sending scorching rays of light down through the leaves.

They took only thirty steps before Hector realised how stupid he was being.

"You've got your phone, right?" he asked. "I bet it has a compass."

"I lost it," she replied, "sometime after getting captured at the camp."

Damn. Hector searched his pockets, hoping his ten-dollar brick might somehow, miraculously, have such a feature. Feeling around for the device, he realised they'd finally had a bit of luck. "Ha! I've still got Ali's phone," he said and whipped it out from the deep zip-up pocket on his hiking trousers.

He tapped the screen, bringing it to life.

"Damn. Only twenty-two percent battery."

"Any signal?"

Hector pursed his lips and shook his head. It was hardly surprising for an uninhabited island. Instead, he flicked on the compass app and glanced up through the trees, looking for a landmark.

"Let's keep the mountain behind us and head this way."

Chapter Twenty-Six

Day Two
13:13
Present Day

After hours of walking, Hector and Anna came across a river, possibly the same one that the soldiers had stopped at, just further down.

Knowing full well it could be contaminated with any number of waterborne diseases, but thirsty enough not to care, Hector drank his fill. He dunked his entire head in it, swallowing the murky, sour-tasting water. It was so cold it was almost icy. *But why?* The sun was blazing, beating the surrounding jungle into extreme temperatures all day, every day.

Anna drank more cautiously at first, scooping up a handful and swilling it around her mouth, trying to decide if it tasted safe. It must have done because she soon joined Hector on his knees.

With hydration, some of the fogginess started to clear from his head. "The river must come out from under the mountain and run down to the lake," he said. "We should be able to follow it right to the water's edge."

Anna nodded and went in for another drink. As she slurped at the water, Hector thought more on their predicament. He soon decided that although there needed to be a time and a place to grieve Ali, Hoa, Ricky, and possibly Em, this sure as hell wasn't it. Their top priority *had to* be getting off this island alive.

Once they did that, Hector realised he would also need to come up with a story plausible enough to explain why they were all missing. Preferably one that wouldn't lead to him spending the rest of his life in some horrific Vietnamese prison or mental asylum. The whole situation was like a nightmare that he kept expecting to wake up from, but never did.

When Anna had drank her fill, the pair pushed onwards. They followed the river as it narrowed and swelled, twisted and turned, heading towards the southernmost tip of the land. After a while, it became apparent that the flow split the island in two and right now it was keeping them from their destination.

"We should cross it soon," Hector called over his shoulder to Anna, who was a few steps behind. The waters had narrowed to a few feet across, and the current didn't look too strong.

Anna agreed, and at a point where there were low-hanging branches to grasp, the pair waded in and dragged themselves through the icy waters, emerging on the far side.

After another two hours of trudging in soaking wet clothes, they found themselves at the rear of the mountain. Here, the forest slowly turned into mangroves. A mesh of roots covered the ground, twisted and knotted together like rogue electrical wires.

The ground grew more waterlogged with each step until it finally disappeared, and the tangle of limbs replaced it as their footholds. The only sounds now seemed to be the chirping of colourful birds overhead and the gentle lapping of the tiny waves around the branches. It was peaceful, almost.

Several times, a flicker of movement in the water close by caught Hector's eye, giving him a stab of panic. Once, he reacted fast enough to see a massive catfish—half his height in length and probably the same in weight—wallowing in the mud before darting off. Two other times, larger and better-camouflaged creatures within the muddy green and brown waters seemed to slide away and disappear just out of sight. After everything they'd been through, Hector certainly didn't want to meet his end being torn to pieces by a freshwater crocodile or constricted to death by a massive reticulated python in the murky shallows.

As they reached the edge of the mangrove forest, the entire southern shoreline came into view. Just a few hundred yards to their right, a patch of rocky ground jutted out into the deep waters.

Hector's heart sank as he realised this must be the only spot that a boat could get close enough to pick them up, and there was no one there. He double-checked the phone's compass and the position of the sun, making sure the mountain was still at their six o'clock in a desperate attempt to prove himself wrong. *No luck.*

The pair clambered over to the cape and walked around at the water's edge, appreciating the solid ground beneath their feet. They would be easily visible standing out in the open, increasing their chances of both getting rescued and getting shot. It was a calculated risk, but one they had to take to be sure there was no boat waiting for them somewhere just out of sight.

As suspected, they found nothing. No distant splutter of engines, no acrid aroma of burning fuel, not even any sign of movement or civilisation upon the distant landscape.

Anna joined Hector, gazing out across the lake with his head hanging. They both dropped sluggishly down to a sitting position a few seconds later.

From here, the top of the water glimmered and sparkled in the afternoon sun, making light of the baking heat. Hector was physically and emotionally drained. His face and neck were sunburnt and sore, his feet were throbbing, and his broken nose made breathing hard and painful.

The pair stood in silence, considering their options for a few minutes.

"What now?" Anna asked, her voice a whisper.

"As far as I can tell, we have two choices. One: we wait here, try to make a signal fire, and probably get shot or die of exhaustion before anyone shows up."

"What's number two?"

"We swim."

It was at least a mile, maybe two, to the nearest stretch of land. He could see the swirling patches of current below the pristine surface. More disconcerting, however, was the quick fade away to blackness.

Hector thought back to the "monsters" Ricky had spoken of, and Van's description of it being "more than just a jungle out there". Having seen more than he ever considered possible over the past two days, he didn't doubt that they were both true.

"What do you think?" he asked.

Anna gave him a sad smile in response, one that still somehow radiated warmth. "I don't know how."

Chapter Twenty-Seven

May 21ˢᵗ

05:50

Fifty-Three Years Ago

One of the neighbours' dogs barking just outside the hut pulled Stanley Rickard from a groggy sleep. Angry voices followed, and the soldier's right hand instinctively slid for his Smith and Wesson. His heart jumped into his throat. It was gone and with it, so was Linh.

Rickard sprang to his feet, ignoring the dizziness. His shoulder was throbbing, but it often did this after a storm. He still wasn't as well as he'd hoped he'd be by now.

The American stumbled towards the ill-fitting wooden door. Just as he was about to reach for the handle, it opened a crack and Linh slid in through the gap.

"Where's my gun?" In his cloudy mind, Rickard had thought for a moment she'd betrayed him. But she wouldn't do that. Not Linh.

"I hid it, and your cigarettes, too."

"Why?" he whispered, although he could already take a pretty decent guess.

"A squad of soldiers from the north arrived," Linh said softly. "They're speaking with my father now."

"Are they looking for me?"

"I don't know. I don't think so. But just in case, I figured it would be better if you weren't armed."

Rickard squeezed her hand. Even though he felt naked without his weapon, she'd done the right thing. Linh gave him a reassuring smile, her beauty making his heart flutter, then slipped back out through the door and quietly pulled it closed.

Outside the long communal village building, Linh watched the men in conversation with her father. The four Northern Vietnamese soldiers looked stern and aggressive, far more so than their counterparts from the south, who were often laughing and joking around.

Linh knew from experience, however, that this was not always the case. Less than a year ago, a squad from the south had utterly decimated a nearby village after finding out one of the elders was feeding information to the Communists. Linh had hardly believed it at first. They'd all just been neighbours, living off the land side by side, until a few years ago.

Now soldiers on both sides were killing men, women and children indiscriminately under the guise of freedom or revenge.

All her people could hope to do was keep their heads down and pray they had chosen the right side when the chips fell.

After a few minutes, the squad leader talking with her father seemed satisfied. He was a skinny man with a sharp, unfriendly face, and the glasses he wore high atop his nose did little to improve his visage. He looked to be only in his mid-twenties, and Linh figured he'd probably got the position through bribery or family connections rather than any proven skills.

As Linh's father spoke, the leader eyeballed him with a look of distaste on his face. After a few seconds, he rose to his feet and led the rest of the squad outside, not even giving the older man a chance to finish his sentence.

Linh's father visibly relaxed, releasing the tension that had seeped into his features over the last few minutes. Her own heart was still beating fast. She wasn't one to scare easily, but for the past few weeks, a new sense of fear, one she'd never felt before, had been growing inside her.

Linh rested a hand on her belly, feeling a gentle flutter that she was sure was a tiny heart beating in time with her own.

"You'll be showing soon," Mai, her teenage sister, had told her a few days before. "You have to tell him, or father, it can't be only me who knows."

"I know," Linh had replied, wanting to avoid the inevitable mayhem that would follow. She had never been one for much drama, preferring to laugh her way through life's problems.

The Northerners worked their way across the rain-soaked yard towards a green flatbed truck that sat at the entrance to the village. Linh smiled and nodded politely as they passed. The squad leader returned the gesture, but his eyes were elsewhere—she could feel them crawling over her body like cockroaches as he walked away. Linh tried her best not to grimace.

A dozen yards from the stone building where her American was hiding, the leader stopped. Linh turned around to face her father. He was smiling, a friendly gesture, trying not to show the cracks of concern that nestled below the surface.

The squad leader bent down and put his fingers into the mud. *What is he doing?*

A moment later, he stood back up, clasping something tiny between his forefingers. A cigarette butt, but not just any cigarette. *A Lucky Strike.*

Linh's father's face dropped. The squad leader drew his pistol and marched back over towards them. The soldiers fell in behind him, Russian machine guns pulled tight to their shoulders. A sudden, overwhelming urge swelled in Linh's stomach. She threw up.

The next hour was by far the worst of his life. Private Stanley Rickard lay with his hands bound, bleeding from the head, while a guard was standing over him, smoking the last of his American cigarettes and smiling smugly. But all this was nothing compared to the sheer torment being experienced by Linh, her kid sister, and her mother as they were each raped and beaten in turn by the Northern Vietnamese soldiers.

When the four men were all finally satisfied, they smacked Rickard around a little more for good measure, then dragged him outside into the humid, grey morning air. The entire village seemed to have disappeared, leaving Linh's family to face the consequences alone. *Fucking pussies.*

Seeing them all on their knees in the mud for saving his life was almost too much to bear. Mai and the girls' mother were both weeping in fear and pain, naked, and covered in blood.

Linh, equally beaten and unclothed, fixed her jaw and stared silently ahead, determined not to cry. Although, it seemed unlikely that even *she* would ever manage a smile again.

"Where are the rest of your squad?" the leader demanded through one of his men, who had passable English. It had been months since Rickard had even seen another American.

"I don't know anything."

"Liar." The leader shot her father.

Rickard ground his teeth so hard they chipped. The screaming and wailing intensified.

"I swear to God, I know nothing. I'm a goddamn deserter!"

The leader shot Linh's mother and moved down the line towards Linh. Her sister had now gone silent, seemingly unable to face the horror of the situation.

"Stop, please," Rickard begged, "I'll tell you everything I know. Take me with you and I'll draw you maps and plans. Everything." They'd soon find out it was a lie and kill him, but at least she'd be safe.

The leader pulled back the hammer on his Chinese-made pistol as though testing Rickard's resolve.

"You can't kill my sister," Mai suddenly begged in her native tongue. "Please, she has a baby."

Rickard knew only a little of the language, but the last word he understood as clear as day, and it cut him deep.

The leader lowered his gun. A curious smile spread across his rat-like face as he muttered something obviously insulting to Linh, no doubt calling her a whore or traitor for carrying a foreigner's bastard.

Linh stared back up at him, her gaze strong and focused, not a hint of shame in her eyes. The squad leader waved for his men to get Rickard up on his feet and turned back towards the truck. They bundled him up onto the cold, damp metal, and the battered diesel engine started to rumble.

The leader walked away. Rickard breathed a sigh of relief. Then, as if he'd forgotten something, the soldier doubled back, whipped his pistol from his belt and fired.

His shot exploded through the front of Linh's head and buried itself in the wet, blood-stained ground behind her. The young woman's body slumped over in the mud, instantly lifeless.

Killing Mai would have been too much of a mercy. Instead, he left the fourteen-year-old girl where she kneeled—orphaned, naked, and crying in the rain alongside the bodies of her entire family. He jogged over to the cab of the truck and casually swung his way up as if he didn't have a care in the world.

Lost in a daze of unspeakable sorrow, Rickard stared back at the scene, bouncing away from him down the dirt road. Linh, her father, her mother, and what would have been his child were dead, all because of him.

With one man at his side, the Rickard could hear the other three soldiers joking and laughing in the cab of the truck, completely unaware or uncaring about the pain they had caused.

Fortunately for Rickard, they were also totally oblivious to the fact that real soon, he was going to murder every single one of them without a shred of mercy or remorse.

Chapter Twenty-Eight

Day Two
15:21
Present Day

"You really can't swim? Not even a little?" Hector asked. It was mind-boggling that anyone in this day and age could lack such a vital skill.

"Maybe a few feet, but that's it. City people like me just don't learn." Anna pursed her lips. "You should go, though. There's no point in us both staying here and probably getting killed. I'll keep searching for Em. Then, maybe you can come back with help?"

Just my luck, Hector thought. *Only I could meet the perfect woman and accidentally lead her directly into a literal incarnation of hell.*

"I know I'm not exactly much use out here," said Hector, "but I can't leave you on your own."

"I'll be okay. I'm not as soft as I look."

"No. It's not happening. We need a new plan."

"Thank you," Anna sighed, obviously relieved, and offered a nervous smile that made her look even more lovely than usual. "Still no signal?"

Hector slid out Ali's phone and tapped the screen. He shook his head, flicking through tabs as if to demonstrate the device's uselessness.

Anna chewed on her lip, lost in thought for a moment. "Maybe the boat driver just got confused," she said eventually. "Ricky asked him to pick the group up on Wednesday morning at first, didn't he? That means he could still come to collect us tomorrow."

Hector shook his head. "I doubt it. The driver took us at the right time, didn't he? He obviously heard nothing from Ricky and left with the money. If we're gonna get out of here alive, it's down to us and us alone."

"What about if we make a raft?"

"It would probably take us days to find enough branches that float and aren't completely rotten. I wish I hadn't dropped that knife."

Anna looked skyward. "Well, whatever happens, we need to find some shelter. A storm's on the way. Get up on your feet."

"How do you know?" Hector asked, clambering up as ordered. He kind of enjoyed hearing her speak with a bit of conviction for once.

"Can't you smell that? The air tastes fresher."

A light breeze was billowing through the trees. There was a clean, watery scent to it that helped lift Hector's spirits.

"Look," she said, leading him a few steps to the right of the jutting-out path until they could see beyond the jungle to the east. A rolling wave of thick, billowing black clouds was working its way towards the island.

The treetops behind them started to rustle and sway. A gust of wind followed, whipping across the valley floor with a haunting howl.

"There could be a good place to stay dry." Hector pointed towards the southern side of the mountain. It didn't look too far from their position and rose steeply from the forest, dotted with black volcanic crags and overhangs.

"Agreed."

It was another half hour before they reached high ground. Under a wide overhang, he and Anna ducked down, finally getting some respite from the winds. They had long since lost their soothing touch.

As Anna swept away some rubble, finding a place to sit, Hector stared out over the vast lake. They'd climbed higher than he'd thought. With that on top of all the walking they'd done today it was no wonder his legs were aching so badly.

The view from this height, however, was almost hypnotising. An immense, solid wall of rain in the distance was hammering the body of water with fury, turning daylight into an almost black shroud of darkness.

When Hector grew tired of the spectacle, he went and sat down beside Anna on a smooth patch of rock. He glanced down at his watch.

"What now?" she said.

"No idea." Hector thought for a while, then raised a finger. "But I know how we can find out," he said. "I'd totally forgotten about this until just now." He pulled Ali's phone out of his pocket. "I think it explains a lot."

Hector held it out and flicked up the brightness on the screen so they could read the report together.

"Wow, where did you find this? It's so accurate," Anna said. "I mean, you saw this one, right? Corporal Truman got shot in the chest exactly as it says. The younger soldier was the interpreter. That leaves Higgs, the black guy, and the sergeant, of course, that one-eyed madman. It looks like everything is happening exactly as it did before."

"Yes." A glimmer of hope came out in Hector's voice as a realisation hit him. "It does... Do you know what that means?"

Anna shrugged, looking baffled at her companion's sudden excitement.

"Well, according to this timeline, everyone will be dead soon after nightfall. Maybe we can just wait it out? It's almost four o'clock now. Sunset is about seven, right? That gives us three hours or thereabouts."

Instead of feeling relieved, Anna looked more troubled than ever, staring down at the mossy roots. "I think so. But surely it can't be that easy?"

"Why not?"

"Well, if they came back once, I'd be willing to bet that they'll come back again. In fact, from what we know so far, I think this has probably been happening every day for more than five decades. A constant cycle of suffering that they can never escape."

How had he missed that? It was so obvious.

"Jesus, you're right. The gunshots we heard on the boat... Ricky said that they repeated every two days. The later ones must have been the girl shooting when we were tied up. It's like a zombie Groundhog Day, beginning from the moment the Americans shoot the first enemy until everyone dies."

"What's a Groundhog Day?"

"The movie. It's a classic. You haven't seen it?"

Anna shrugged and pursed her lips. Even in spite of everything, she was beautiful.

"I guess not. Was it like this?"

Hector grimaced. "Not exactly. It had a happy ending for a start. Once Phil finally made…" He trailed off as the gears rotated in his head. For some reason though, he still felt as if he was missing the big picture.

"What is it?"

"I just thought of something," Hector said. "But it's not important."

The storm was getting closer with each second, its volume swelling to a distant roar. Hector glanced down at his feet, mud-caked and sore.

"So, what do we do now?" Anna asked.

"What *can* we do? I write bullshit travel articles and you're a fashion editor—no offense. We don't belong here, so we should just stay clear and let them all kill each other. Then hopefully we can find a way off the island before it all starts again."

Anna sighed, the expression on her face was one of exasperation. She reached out and took his hand. "I know you're afraid. I am too, but you've seriously got to give yourself some credit here. You're the only reason we're still alive after facing those *things.*" She shuddered at the thought.

She could be right, Hector thought. He'd at least tried to fight Rickard when he attacked Ali. Even if it was too little too late. For some reason, he always torpedoed himself like this. It was why he hadn't got a girlfriend, why he had nothing but a few crappy travel articles to show after a decade of trying to make it as a journalist. *Well no more.*

"If it makes any difference, I'm a fraud too," Anna continued.

"A fraud? What do you mean?"

"I don't really know anything about fashion or lifestyle. Mine and Em's families are both dirt poor. We both just pretend to be rich and stylish… maybe hoping some of it would rub off on us."

Hector smiled. "Well, you had me fooled."

"None of that really matters now anyway."

"Probably not."

"We won't survive a second round, will we?" she asked, looking almost as depressed as he felt.

"No, I'm sure we could, if we really had to."

Hector tried his best to sound convincing. Anna wasn't buying it but seemed to appreciate the sentiment, nonetheless. She pushed up closer to him until their thighs were touching. *Probably for warmth.*

"Do you think the others will come back too? Ricky, Ali, and Hoa I mean."

Hector thought better than pointing out that Em was likely already dead, too.

"God, I *really* hope not." He pondered the question for a moment before continuing. "I just keep thinking th—"

Anna leaned in and pushed her lips against his own.

Before he even had a chance to question what was happening, he was lost in the warmth of her kiss and the feel of her soft skin pressed against his own. His nose throbbed, and he struggled to breathe, but it was easily worth the pain.

After a few seconds, she pulled back, smiling.

"What was that for?" He grinned like a giddy schoolboy.

"Well, it doesn't look like we're going to live much longer, does it? Besides, we have a connection, don't we?" she said. "I mean, I like you Hector, and I'm pretty sure that you feel the same way about me."

Even in the dim light, he was a little too conscious of his face burning red and decided to own the fact. "Yeah. That's right."

"Well, in that case, let's do this. I don't want to die a virgin."

"A what?!" He could hardly believe his ears. Surely that wasn't possible? She was way too attractive to be a virgin.

Without a response, Anna slipped off her muddy, sweat-stained shirt to reveal a black sports bra that looked like it was barely able to contain its contents.

Only after a second of stunned silence did Hector finally snap out of his trance. This had been a very weird and depressing day. But it seemed like things were now about to improve, drastically.

"Wow. Okay, sure. But give me a minute?" he said. "I have to… I have to pee."

She laughed nervously. "Hurry, it's getting cold."

Nodding with fervour, Hector bounded to his feet and marched out of the outcrop to see the rains already pounding down like a thick black sheet on the forest below them.

He walked a few yards up, wondering how the hell he ever ended up here, and found a patch far enough away that she wouldn't be able to see or hear him. All the while, shaking his head in disbelief.

There was a small stream running down beside him. *Maybe I should have a quick wash?* The last couple of days had been hot and sticky, to say the least. Taking care of his hygiene would just be a common courtesy.

Chapter Twenty-Nine

Day Two
16:02
Fifty Years Ago

With the exception of a single stop to drink from a stream, Sang had been walking for almost nine hours. Her feet had blistered, those blisters had burst, and were now patches of raw pink skin and bloody scabs.

The recycled rubber sandals that the army supplied were efficient for stopping infection, allowing such wounds to get air to them rather than stewing and rotting under thick material. But Sang's were a good inch too big for her. They rubbed and chafed in half a dozen places with each step.

Unfortunately, it wasn't just her feet that were causing problems. Sang's legs were like stone, weighing her down and causing her to stumble clumsily from one step to the next. It was only a matter of time before she damaged a knee, an ankle, or worse. Meanwhile, the straps of her gun and the heavy backpack, laden with supplies, cut deep into her shoulders.

Sang's whole body was screaming in pain, aching for rest, but inside she was numb. Losing the only man she'd ever truly loved had left a mark on her soul as dark as the caves they called home.

If it wasn't for the others that needed her, Sang would probably have given up already. It was almost too tempting just to lie down on the forest floor and weep, or, even better, put a bullet in her head and be done with the pain and suffering of this life.

No. You have to do it for Ly, she told herself. *You promised to take her away from here.*

Sang didn't know how long it would be before the soldiers found the outpost, they were already getting close. Hopefully, her gambit, leading them on a wild goose chase round the island, would buy the inhabitants of Hill Two Fourteen a few more hours at least. However, persuading Captain Chien, Huy, and Grandma Lan that they needed to flee, once she finally made it back, would be a different matter.

On the steep, rocky southern side of the mountain, Sang abandoned everything but her gun. She hid her backpack in a hollow beneath a tree that jutted out from the hillside towards sunlight.

It would be far easier for her to scramble up the outcrops with minimal equipment than it would for the soldiers with their heavy loads. From the look of the leader's short limbs and compact, muscular frame, she figured he wasn't much of a natural climber. *Hopefully, he'll slip and break his neck.*

Within the hour, Sang found her way to a familiar animal trail that led up to the caves. She had never seen the creatures that left the tracks but had once noticed a pair of large glowing yellow eyes, watching her and Truong as they walked hand in hand through a cool spring night.

That evening in particular he had been on watch, so they'd set up a mosquito net-covered hammock amongst a patch of trees and slept wrapped around each other as a husband and wife should. That perfect night had been one of far too few.

Sang gritted her teeth as a wave of despair washed over her, knowing she would never have the chance to do so again. But somehow, she found the strength to press on.

By the time she reached the entrance to the caves, the storm clouds had closed in and were on the verge of breaking. In the low light, Sang pressed her body against the warm, damp stone and edged carefully around the traps.

Entering the tunnel, the humid summer evening fell away and a wall of icy cold air hit her, thick with the musky scents of bat faeces and mould. She despised this place; it was a prison, but it was still her home. Sang resolved that she would either leave today a free woman, taking Ly with her, or die defending it.

With the end of her journey in sight, cold, dehydration, and exhaustion soon caught up. Sang was shivering so violently that she could barely stand. Despite this, fear that the Americans might have reached the caverns before her, and what she would find if they had, forced her feet to keep moving.

Rather than losing her head, Sang focused on the constant and calming sound of water rushing alongside the tunnel, somewhere beyond the cracks and crevices to her right.

After another fifteen minutes of climbing and clambering, the flickering yellow lamps that lined the tunnel and main cavern came into view. They cast long strange shadows across the floor and hurt her eyes with their glare, but they were a wonderful sight.

The moment Sang entered, however, she could tell something was wrong. On the far side of the cavern, fifteen feet from the barracks, there was a semi-circle of sandbags that the two once-soldiers must have dragged into the alcove. A pair of rifle barrels poked over the top, aiming directly at her.

As Sang stepped into the light, Chien rose from behind the fortification.

"Sang? You scared the hell out of us," he said, letting the weapon hang over his stump. "Here, you look like you need this." He paced towards her, awkwardly unclipping a canteen from his belt and passed it to her. She dropped to the ground where she stood and quickly finished the bottle.

"We didn't think you were coming back," Chien continued. "Where are the others?"

She shook her head, eyes fixed on the ground, unable to look him in the eye.

"Oh my God... All of them?"

"Truong and Long," she answered, biting her lip. "I think I lost the soldiers for now, but we need to blow the tunnel and get out of here before they pick up my trail."

"Oh dear," the old soldier said, his wrinkled face wearing a grim expression. One that she knew all too well.

"What's wrong?"

"It's Ly. She's been gone since this afternoon. We thought you'd taken her with you."

"Why in God's name would I do that?" Sang shot back up. "We have to look for her... right now." Suddenly her feet no longer hurt, her back no longer ached.

"It's too dangerous. If the American squad are as close as you say, we may end up leading them right back here. We need to follow through with the contingency plan, blow up the tunnel and get as many of us as we can out of here in the boat."

"NO!" Sang took a breath, biting back her anger at the heartless old man. "Please give me two hours? They won't attack us until nightfall anyway, that's what Truong said. Even if they do, then you can set off the charges and leave without us."

"I'll give you one hour. Then, we have no choice. The Americans can't know what we've been doing here—stockpiling weapons and hiding our troops' movements—or else it'll expose our whole operation."

"Thank you." Sang's voice trembled. "One hour. I'll find her, I promise."

Chapter Thirty

Day Two
16:05
Present Day

Am I really going to do this? Anna wondered. *Why the heck not?* She'd already been suppressing her desires for too long already, waiting for the right man who never seemed to come along.

If the last couple of days had taught her anything, it was that life was fragile and worth living well while you still had the chance. Besides, Hector was better than every other shallow idiot her friends had tried to set her up with before. He was good-looking too, not Hollywood good-looking, but he had one of those faces that you could tell straight away belonged to someone nice. That was more important.

Anna waited at the mouth of the shallow cave for his return. It didn't take long for her to become transfixed by the storm, watching it thunder down across the coast of the island. The summer rains always had that effect on her. There was something special about the way they could conjure such power with nothing but a taste in the air and a distant rumble from the heavens as a warning.

As a girl, she used to stare out of her apartment window for hours sometimes, watching the rains pound the blue tarpaulin sheets that covered the street market opposite. They would clear the dust and refresh the atmosphere, returning a sense of balance to the world.

Movement to Anna's right told her that Hector was back. She turned towards him, feeling surprisingly calm considering what was about to happen.

"What?!" She jumped in shock and stumbled back into the cover of the overhang. "Oh my God!" Anna clutched her hands to her chest. Her heart was pounding beneath them, as though it was trying to burst free.

At the edge of the entrance, half hidden by the darkness of the tropical storm, stood the last figure she had ever expected to see.

The stranger was wearing heavy military fatigues that had obviously been altered to better fit her. The skinny little girl couldn't have been more than three or four years old.

She grinned at Anna, looking strangely pleased with herself. Strings of sodden, long black hair clumped together and stuck to her cheeks like spiderwebs. The taken-in uniform was dripping wet, even though the rains had yet to reach this far inland. The child's face was white as snow, with the exception of dark shadows around her sunken eyes and purple lips. Anna shuddered, trying to hide her expression of horror and repulsion.

"They're here. See, I told you," the deceased little girl called happily over her shoulder.

"What?" Anna asked. "What are you doing out here all by yourself?"

"I'm not by myself. See…"

A moment later, Em stumbled up behind the child. Her hair was dishevelled and muddy, her face grotesquely swollen, covered with black and purple bruises, her nose off at an angle, and her lips double their normal size.

"Em? You're alive!" Anna ran over, forgetting about being shirtless, and wrapped her arms around her friend's neck.

"I'm so glad to see you," Em said, or tried to say at least, only then revealing that she was missing most of her teeth at the front.

"What happened to you? No. Don't speak. Rest. Do you need water?"

Em nodded and Anna started looking outside for Hector, hoping he could find something to drink nearby.

"Is it that bad?" Em asked, barely able to form the words, and put a hand to her face. She recoiled at the disfigurement, clenching her eyes shut with anger. Her modelling career was certainly over.

"Have you seen *Chi Sang*?" the girl said in Vietnamese, using the pronoun which meant big sister. "She hasn't come back. I went to find her, but I met your friend instead."

With Hector nowhere to be seen, Anna supported Em over her shoulders and helped carry her deeper into the shelter. "Err, what does she look like?" Anna asked. She turned back and jumped on reflex, not realising the child had followed her in and was now standing just an inch to her rear.

Caught somewhere between fear and maternal instinct, Anna raised a hand to show she was no threat.

"Her name is Sang. You'll know it's her because she's so pretty."

"Oh. I'm sorry, sweetheart. We haven't seen your sister. What's your name?"

"Ly."

"Where did you come from, Ly?"

"I live up there." She waved a hand lazily towards the hillside.

"You live on the mountain?"

"Nope," she giggled. "We don't live on the mountain, we live *in* the mountain."

"Who's we?"

"Me, Sang, Grandma Lan, Captain Chien—he has one arm, Huy—he can't speak, and Khai—he's still my friend, even though he's a big boy."

A sharp pain, like the stab of a needle, forced its way through Anna's chest. The young girl was so much like her own younger sister had been at that age, it was shocking. Now, at sixteen, Quynh was a typical teenager, constantly arguing with her siblings and prone to massive emotional outbursts, but she used to be so sweet and happy, like Ly.

"What happened to you? Why are you all wet? Did you get caught in the storm?"

"What storm?" The girl answered. "No. I never go outside."

"But you're soaked?"

Ly pinched her shirt with a tiny finger and thumb, watching it drip in puzzlement. "Oh, so I am." She giggled. "I don't know why. Anyway, if you see my sister, please tell her to come back. I've got a new game to play. I've been waiting for her *all* day."

As Ly spoke, Anna put two and two together, blaming the exhaustion and hunger for her slow thoughts. "Maybe we *did* see her. She's a soldier too, right? And tucks her hair up under her hat."

"Yes! That's her. She's the only girl soldier."

"I remember now." Anna tried to smile, choking on the lump in her throat. The young woman with the vicious stab wounds in her abdomen had saved their lives by throwing them her folding knife before taking off through the forest like a cat. "I think she was coming back this way."

"Oh, good." A grin broke though on the child's purple lips. "I'm going to look for her, even though Grandma Lan says I'm not allowed to go out on my own."

"She sounds wise."

"She is. But Sang is my favourite. One day we're going to live outside together. She's not my real sister. I just call her that because she's like a big sister to me."

"That's lovely," Anna answered, choked up while staring into the bloodshot eyes of the long-dead little girl.

"If you see her, go up that way," Ly said, pointing to a path that headed east, round towards the top of the mountain. "Look for the teeny-tiny hole about halfway up. But don't fall into the traps, they're for the bad guys."

"Traps?"

She nodded, her clumped wet hair sticking to her face. "Yes. They're really pointy. Okay. Bye."

Ly spun on her heels and ran out of shelter.

"Wait," Anna called. She quickly lowered Em to the floor and ran out behind the child. However, all she saw was Ly's back disappearing up over the rocks as she clambered up the hillside. *Oh no.*

Chapter Thirty-One

Day Two
16:11
Present Day

Here we go.

Hector took a deep breath and climbed down past the overhang to the mouth of the shelter. "Alright, I'm ready to d— Em? You're okay!"

The rush of elation at seeing Em alive was sharply followed by guilt. She looked anything but 'Okay'. Disappointment wasn't far behind either when he realised the ship had likely sailed with Anna.

"Hector!" she tried to shout, but it came out more like *Hethor*, her face showing what could have been happiness.

He grimaced at the swollen mess. One eye was puffed up to nearly twice its size. Her lips were swollen so badly, it looked like she had a botched Botox treatment. Meanwhile, Em's mouth was full of pointed, broken teeth that, coupled with her puffy-yet-bony complexion, made her look like one of those deep-sea fish with stretched faces and razor-like fangs.

"Are you alright?" He asked.

She nodded in response, looking pretty damn cheery, all things considered. Maybe it was from the flicker of hope she now felt after spending the last twenty-four hours lost, injured, and alone.

"How did you find us? Where's Anna?"

Em pointed over to the western side of the mountain and her friend appeared at the entrance, almost on cue. Anna was still in her sports bra, panting hard and red-faced, as though she'd run a mile uphill. *Damn*, she was hot though, and he'd missed the chance by a matter of minutes.

Hector gave Anna a few moments to catch her breath. Meanwhile, the blanket of rain erupted overhead. Huge tropical droplets crashed into the hillside, throwing the musky scents of warm earth and damp vegetation into the air.

Anna wiped her face down with her shirt and slipped it back on over her head as a shudder ran through her.

"It was a girl," she said at last, still panting. "A kid, looking for her sister. The one who threw me the knife."

"Back up a minute," Hector said. "There's someone else on the island? Not just soldiers?"

Em nodded frantically, grunting in reply through her smashed jaw and giving him a thumbs up like he had won the world's most messed up game of charades.

"Oh my God... How many people?"

"It wasn't clear. But she mentioned a grandma and one other kid, at least. Oh, and the woman who threw me the knife earlier, she called her Sang."

"That's it." Everything clicked into place. Of course, this wasn't just about soldiers killing each other—that always happened in war. *How could I have been so stupid?*

"Remember the message in Hoa's book, talking about the innocent people and asking her to set them free?" Hector said. "And what you and Ricky told us about how the terrible fates were only for those who had suffered tragedies, right?"

"Yes." Anna looked like she was following, but with some sense of apprehension. "But those stories aren't supposed to be literal. A hungry ghost is like purgatory, souls that live in continuous suffering, unable to move on, starving for eternity."

"Well, can you think of anything worse than living and dying in a battle you don't believe in, watching your friends or family die around you while you can do nothing to help them, again and again, forever?"

"When you put it like that..."

Hector could see tears welling in the corners of Anna's eyes, and he suddenly resented the example, thinking of Ali, Ricky, and Hoa dying. He forced the feeling down, swallowed hard, and continued.

"Hoa wanted to find her brother's remains to stop his suffering, right?"

She nodded.

"Well, right now, the remains of everyone who died here are up and walking about, armed to the teeth and trying to murder each other, so that's obviously not the answer."

"Well..." Anna looked at him, pursing her lips, looking unsure where he was going with this and equally uncertain she would want to find out. "What do you think *is* the answer, then?"

"When the girl, Sang, shot that soldier earlier, she hit the exact place of his wounds and he died. But when Ali tried to shoot the sergeant, it did nothing."

"Yes, but—"

"So, it's like a time loop," Hector said, desperate not to lose his train of thought. "These things have already happened, like the wound in his eye. That's how he was supposed to die. How he did, and still does, die. That's why Ali couldn't kill him. I bet that's why they couldn't keep following us too. They have to complete their mission, exactly the same as it happened before."

"So, there's nothing we can do?"

A glimmer in Hector's eye said otherwise. "Not necessarily. Maybe we've been looking at this the wrong way. What if, rather than us trying to change things ourselves, we could get *them* to do something different?"

Anna blinked a few times, wrapping her thoughts around his idea. "That doesn't sound very realistic. You saw what the sergeant was like." She thought for a moment. "On the other hand, we *do* know exactly when and where the battle takes place. Maybe we could persuade the civilians just to leave before they even arrive?"

"YES!" Hector was practically shouting over the volume of the pounding rains. "This is the way out of this mess. I'm sure of it!"

"But Hector…" Anna's voice was shaking. "They already died, decades ago. Nothing we can do can change that. It's impossible."

"Frankly, this whole damn ordeal is impossible. But I didn't just spend the last two days being hunted down by a literal zombie army, watching my friends die, for all this to be meaningless." Hector's voice softened as he met Anna's eyes. "If there's a chance that we can break this cycle and save all of our lives in the process, then we have to try."

Anna held his gaze, impressed by his conviction. She glanced back at Em, who nodded in response with an expression that seemed to say, 'what have I got to lose?'

Hector swallowed, trying not to dwell on the doubts in the back of his mind, or the fear of what they might face in the caves.

"Better go quick then," Anna said. "It's gonna be a long walk and we don't have much time."

Chapter Thirty-Two

Day Two
17:22
Present Day

As the deluge lashed the surrounding hillside, the path turned into a river. Slick mud and floating deadwood almost took Hector out more than once.

Anna led the way, following the route she'd seen Ly take. Em trudged behind her, and Hector followed in the rear with his eyes on stalks, knowing the Americans could take them by surprise at any moment.

After a while, the storm started to soften. With fewer immediate dangers occupying his thoughts, Hector could start mentally preparing himself for what was coming. He glanced skywards, wishing he could see the sun to get an idea of how long they had until nightfall. *If the timeline from the report is right, it'll be less than two hours by now.*

The trail soon opened up into a thin plateau that backed onto a wall of solid rock. The space was twenty feet across, but double that in length.

Anna paused, scanning the wall, then stopped. Hector followed her gaze towards a crack in the stone on their left. It was just four feet high, obscured with dangling vines, and looked like nothing but another overhang. He figured that was probably the point. They'd seen similar features all over the mountain.

He took a step toward it. "Wait," Anna said, putting an arm across his chest. "There are traps."

Just three paces ahead, the leaf-covered ground rose slightly. On closer inspection, Hector discovered a layer of thin sticks that would have easily given way under his weight.

"Thanks," he said, both disturbed and impressed by Anna and the four-year-old girl's combined knowledge of guerrilla warfare tactics.

The group edged through the forest around the traps until they were almost opposite the small opening. As they were about to start picking a route through, a rustling in the nearby trees caught Hector's attention.

"Stop," he whispered with his palm raised, pressing back into the cover of the forest, urging Anna and Em to do the same.

A crackle of radio static hissed from the bushes directly opposite the cave entrance, barely audible over the patter of raindrops on leaves and the distant growls of thunder.

The figure that had once been Watts, the interpreter, crept out from the foliage, his body still covered in sickening puncture wounds. "I, err... I think I have a location here, sir. Over," he said into his radio, trying to sound like a real soldier.

"You *think*?" Rickard's familiar southern drawl crackled through the speaker. "I need confirmation."

Hector stood like a statue, watching the young interpreter take cautious steps forward.

Watts put one foot on the first layer of the branches and quickly withdrew, apparently noticing the change in sensation beneath his feet. He kicked aside the layer of foliage that revealed a brutal pit of sharpened bamboo rods. Watts clicked the radio again.

"They're here, sir, I'm sure. Three sets of tracks led right up to an entrance in the hillside. Should I investigate? Over."

Hector hissed a curse under his breath. Had the three of them just guided the American squad right to the civilians? If so, his well-intentioned plan may have done more harm than good.

"Negative."

Both Watts and Hector breathed a simultaneous sigh of relief.

"Return to rendezvous to gear up for full assault."

That bastard. Rickard clearly had no intention of only doing reconnaissance, despite his orders. Whether it was the dream of glory, revenge, or pure bloodlust that compelled the sergeant, Hector couldn't be sure. But one way or another, they needed to be out of there before sundown.

Rather than following orders, Watts checked around him to make sure he wasn't being watched, then reached into his jacket pocket.

The interpreter pulled out a plastic wallet containing an almost-brown letter. He ducked back under the cover of the thick leaves, taking shelter from the gently falling rain, and carefully unfolded the letter with spindly fingers.

Watts slumped against the nearest tree with his back towards Hector, Anna, and Em, giving his watchers a good view over his shoulder. Although it was too far away to make out any of the words, Hector could see the letter was hand-written in faded black ink, the paper itself weathered and worn. The young soldier stared down, reading for a couple of minutes.

What the hell is he doing? Hector wondered, watching from the undergrowth.

Watts began to cry. He muttered a few words under his breath, trying to keep his sobbing to a minimum. Hector couldn't help but feel a little sympathy for the young man, so far from home and so out of place. Living this nightmare again and again, dying every second night, and returning to suffer again the next morning.

With trembling fingers, Watts reached in behind the letter and took out a faded black-and-white image. He held up the photo in front of his face. Between layers of mud, water, blood, and bleached by decades of sunlight, the picture had almost disappeared entirely.

The face of a smiling baby girl and a laughing mother holding her were just about visible. Watts looked proud, as though he was still seeing the image as it once had been.

Could it be a daughter? Maybe a little sister? The girl was probably grown, maybe even a mother or grandmother herself. Still, it was heart-breaking to know the interpreter may have never had the chance to meet her. *Maybe he still can?* There was no way to know how this — whatever it was — worked.

Watts eventually put the photo back, folded the letter up, and then tucked the package back into his top pocket, buttoning it to ensure the safety of its precious contents. He wiped the tears from his face, smearing them with the back of his sleeve and checking his appearance with a shaving mirror from his belt to make sure he looked like he hadn't been crying.

Rickard would probably shoot him right then and there if he knew. The sergeant was undoubtedly a merciless bastard. Higgs appeared as if he could go either way. He didn't seem to take any pleasure in killing from what they'd seen, but certainly didn't have any qualms about doing his job. This young man, however, didn't belong in a war zone any more than a pair of fashionistas or a fluff-piece travel writer did.

Watts climbed wearily back to his feet, and rather than returning to the rendezvous as ordered, he entered the small clearing and stood before the same trap that had nearly taken Hector out. The translator stayed there for a minute, staring with dread at the obscured false floor. It was almost as if he remembered the fate that awaited him on some level.

"We have to slow them down," Anna whispered.

She was right, of course, and if the dozens of stab wounds that littered Watts's body were anything to go on, this was where his mission ended. Even so, the thought of pushing the soldier into the trap made Hector feel physically ill.

As if reading his thoughts, Anna tapped him on the shoulder and nodded towards the hole. He shook his head. Watts *needed* to go in, but it didn't have to be now. Making the wrong move would likely just speed up the assault, cutting their already narrow window of opportunity back even further.

Obviously not picking up the same clues, Em barged past him. "Pussy," she hissed as best she could while missing most of her teeth and broke into a flat-out sprint.

The once-model caught her foot on a root after just five feet and half ran, half fell the next ten, finally barrelling into Watts's back and sending him flying face first towards the spikes.

His arms flapped and flailed in desperation, trying to find anything that would stop his descent. Unfortunately for the interpreter, the pit was wide enough that no hand holds even came close.

Watts's horrific scream burst through the trees, followed by a morbid crunch as twenty razor-sharp bamboo rods simultaneously impaled his face, chest, and legs. Watts's ability to produce anything more than a whimper soon disappeared, and Hector tried his best to block the sights, sounds, and smells from his mind.

"THAT'S FOR RUINING MY FUCKING FACE!" Em screamed semi-comprehensibly at the dying man. Even though he'd only been a bystander to her beating, she had a look of manic joy in her eyes upon being able to extract some small measure of revenge.

Watts's radio immediately crackled to life down below. "Was that you, Private? We're moving to your position now. Over."

Hector swung Em round by the shoulder, still feeling repelled by the severe swelling on her face. She shrugged. "Someone had to do it."

"You may well have just ruined everything," Hector said, unsure if he was furious at her for putting them in even more danger, or if he was overjoyed that she had proved that they did indeed have some influence over how the battle played out. Only as he averted his gaze skywards from the grim scene did Hector realise how quickly the light was fading. "We need to get moving fast."

Chapter Thirty-Three

Day Two
17:47
Present Day

Soon after they entered the cave, the storm picked back up to full force. Howling winds and torrents of rain whipped the rock face overhead. Although it was a relief not to be exposed, the perfectly still and numbingly cold air inside wasn't much more welcoming.

Thirty yards from the entrance, the pathway took a steep downward angle. Hector went first, trying, and failing, to make a controlled descent. After the first few feet, he lost grip and slid down the rocky slope, landing hard in a pool of muddy water at the bottom. It gave him the eerie feeling of being swallowed into the belly of some vast stone leviathan.

At this depth, the gurgle of rainwater flowing across the mountainside overhead was muffled and distant. Outside, wiry fingers of lightning burst across the sky and momentarily lit up the tunnel as bright as day. The accompanying thunder was nearly instant; a massive explosion of noise so loud it literally shook the mountain.

The brief flash of light left Hector's eyes straining in the dark. But also reminded him that Ali's phone was still in his front pocket. Luckily, it had stayed dry.

Hector pulled it out and tapped the torch icon. A still single pale LED flicked to life, giving the group their first consistent view of their surroundings. It was a long, winding lava tube that twisted and turned away further than he could see into the shadows.

"Six percent," Hector said. "It won't last long. Have you got your phone, Em?"

"It's dead."

"Maybe it'll come back to life in a few hours." Anna said, bringing a smile to his lips.

They walked as fast as the darkness and the awkward pathway would allow, having to duck and crawl on all fours through gaps no bigger than waist height every few minutes.

Finally, the tunnel opened up, becoming ten feet wide and more than thirty high. A living ceiling of bats that must have numbered in the hundreds of thousands lined the roof. The ground was slick beneath Hector's feet and the sour, pungent stench of guano filled the air.

With the sound of footsteps, more and more of the creatures awoke and started swarming. They flew erratically within inches of Hector, Anna, and Em's faces, as if intentionally trying to freak them out.

Keeping his eyes focused on the path ahead and trying to ignore the bats, Hector felt something crunch beneath his foot. He couldn't help but take a peek, although he immediately regretted the decision.

The creature on the ground was like something out of a nightmare. A red-bodied giant centipede, with spindly yellow legs, almost the size and width of his forearm, was half crushed beneath his foot. It thrashed and pulled, eventually tearing its front half away from the flat rear section, and scuttled off into the darkness.

The path narrowed again and they then turned a corner that completely cut them off from any remaining light. To make matters worse, Ali's phone bleeped its final warning. Hector had just enough time to get a glimpse at the clock before it shut down completely, plunging the motley crew into absolute blackness.

"Six-fourteen," Hector said. "We still have about forty-five minutes until nightfall."

"Erm, no we don't," Em answered.

"What do you mean, we don't?"

She took a deep breath, knowing the effort of explaining would cause her significant pain. "Sunset today is at six thirty-two. It was seven most of last month. We've got, like, seventeen minutes."

Both Anna's and Hector's mouths fell open. Not that they could see each other. "What? How do you know that?"

"I always know when it's sunset."

"Why?!" he could barely believe what he was hearing.

She shrugged and sheepishly answered, "Best time of day for selfies."

"Jesus. Why didn't you say anything before?"

"I thought you knew."

Hector put his head in his hands and took a few deep breaths, trying to control his rising panic.

"This is a goddamn disaster," he said, letting his words sink in. *It's exactly what I get for trusting my gut.*

With no idea what lay ahead, but certain it must be better than coming face to face with the crazed sergeant in the pitch-black tunnel, Hector picked up the pace. With his arms outstretched, navigating as much by the feel of stone beneath his hands and feet as he was with vision, he led the group in a blind charge forward.

Round the next bend in the path, the acrid scents of wood smoke and diesel hit his nostrils. Soon after, a distant string of lamps came into view. They cast a warm yellow glow along the right-hand side of the tunnel, giving the illusion of it being some kind of nineteenth century coal mine.

Hector released a slow, relieved breath as the group entered the main cavern. A sense of awe at the sheer scale of the space soon overtook what remained of his angst. It was like some vast, ancient castle hall, a hundred feet across and double that in height.

Through the dim light, Hector struggled to make out the far walls. Around the outside of the cavern, stalactites sagged down from the ceiling and stalagmites jutted up from the floor. Together, they gave the impression that the huge cavern was slowly melting and dripping like candle wax around them.

To their right, beyond the long string of lamps, was a pathway. It led down towards a narrow ledge that dropped off again after just ten feet, to what sounded like a powerful underground river. It didn't take a genius to figure out how the soaked little girl Anna spoke with had met her end.

The left-hand side of the cavern sloped upwards to a stepped plateau. In its centre was a massive stack of tarpaulin-covered crates. The manpower that it must have taken to carry in this quantity of supplies was phenomenal.

Hector followed the shadowy walls to the furthest corner, and towards what looked like a rusty tin shed. To the side of the decrepit structure was a low stack of mouldy green sandbags covered with lichen and moss. Behind the fortification, two figures, barely visible in the darkness, trained rifles on them, but seemed apprehensive about shooting.

"Hands on your head," one man shouted in a strained, weak voice, trying to command authority. His accent was thick, but Hector didn't need him to repeat himself and slowly raised both hands.

Anna answered back in Vietnamese. The voice shouted again, more weathered and agitated than before. Even for Hector, who didn't know a word of his language, the desperation in the defender's tone was obvious.

An older man in uniform rose from behind the sandbags a second later and paced towards the group. The barrel of a Kalashnikov was supported over his handless right arm. The entire right-hand side of this soldier's face, from the jaw up, was gone, carved out in an odd circular gap like a missing puzzle piece. In its place was a mass of congealed, rotted flesh and brain, black and putrefied, crawling with maggots. Even from twenty feet, the stench was utterly overpowering.

Anna begged, "Please, we have t—"

The half-faced soldier barked his order again.

Just as Hector started to speak, a clunk of metal echoed through the cavern and cut him short. He swung his head towards the sound, in time to see a gas canister come bouncing across the ground and stop near his feet.

With a hiss, it expelled a flow of noxious, yellow smoke. A burning signal flare then landed to its side, illuminating the cavern with a streaked red hue of light, like some kind of nightmarish, underground nightclub. *This was a terrible mistake.*

Chapter Thirty-Four

Day Two
18:16
Fifty Years Ago

Sang's heart was pounding as she clambered back through the tunnel with reckless abandon, praying she wasn't too late. The search outside had been useless, and the only thing keeping Sang going was the hope that Ly had returned while she was gone.

A minute later, the outline of a lone figure came into view, creeping down the tunnel less than fifty feet ahead. Sang whipped Ares from her bloody shoulder and took aim, holding it steady as she closed the gap.

The unknown walker stepped into the lamplight near the end of the tunnel and Sang realised then they were too small to be one of the American soldiers.

"Ly?" she called out.

"Big sister, is that you?" The little girl spun round. Her eyes were wide, staring blindly into the darkness.

"Yes, it is me." A sweeping wave of relief crashed into Sang, followed a second later by Ly, who ran full speed into her with her arms extended to an embrace. The impact sent jolts of pain through Sang's back and legs, making her feel as though the events of the day had aged her the better part of a century.

Sang hugged Ly tight, stroking the back of her head. "Where were you going?" she scolded. "You scared me."

"I went to find you. Grandma Lan told me not to, but I wanted to help. You're my best friend and, well… I love you."

Sang kneeled down to get to Ly's level, overjoyed to see the smile on her face. "You could have got hurt," she said, letting out a delirious laugh. "You're a very brave little sister, and I love you a lot. But if anything ever happens to me, I need you to promise that you'll run away. You don't come back looking for me, okay?"

The little girl's lip quivered. "What's going to happen to you?"

"I don't know," Sang replied, running her fingers through Ly's long black hair, watching as it glimmered like polished coal in the darkness. "Just promise me."

"I promise."

"Now. Quick, we need to get back. Everyone's leaving soon." Sang snatched Ly up, sitting her on her hip, and slung Ares over the other shoulder.

"Really? Where are we going?"

"I don't know yet. But it'll be exciting, a real adventure."

"But there's a big storm. Is that okay?"

"It'll have to be."

Sang shouted over to Captain Chien as she entered the cavern. He waved back, looking relieved, but didn't stop his preparations, piling more sandbags up around the alcove on the southern wall. Time was of the essence, after all.

A long brown wire ran from near her feet over to the improvised fortification. If all went to plan, he and Huy would bring down the last hundred yards of the tunnel with strategically placed charges and take out the entire American squad in one go.

The thought of knowingly sealing oneself inside the mountain, however, made Sang shudder.

According to Chien, the boat couldn't fit more than four without risking a capsize. So he and Huy would find an alternative route out through one of the hundred or more tiny passages that led away from the cavern. Although, whether the invalid and the old captain could reach the outside before oxygen, water, food, or all three ran out, was a different matter altogether.

"Can I bring my dolls?" Ly asked. Sang glanced towards the barracks, knowing she couldn't deprive the girl of the only remaining memento of her father.

"Khai," Sang called to the lanky twelve-year-old who was helping Captain Chien and Huy with their final checks. He came running over. "Take Ly to find her toys—I think one of them was on the table—then help her and Grandma Lan down into the boat. We're leaving in three minutes."

The boy gave her a quick salute and ran off, dragging Ly by the hand. Sang glanced down towards the water's edge where the boat was moored, clacking against the wall, buffeted by the underground current. Grandma Lan was already at the top of the ladder, packing emergency rations and medical supplies into a green military backpack. *At least we're well prepared for them.*

Sang reloaded her rifle from a metal ammo box on the weapons rack. She dropped a few extra rounds into her pocket and, in doing so, realised that she'd lost the folding knife from her belt.

In need of a replacement fast, Sang grabbed a machete from the rack and tied the wooden case onto her waist with yarn. These home-made hunting blades were simple pig iron, but they were fire-hardened and sharpened until they became the perfect tool for hacking through either the jungle or the body of an enemy soldier.

Pushing aside her fear, Sang jogged back over towards Captain Chien and Huy, who were preparing their rifles behind the sandbags, and saluted them.

The former officer returned her gesture with an awkward left-handed salute and shook her hand. "Take care of those kids," Chien said, nodding over to the group waiting at the top of the rope ladder. "Heaven knows they've been through enough."

"I will, sir." She shook Huy's hand, and he nodded in response, suddenly more lucid and purposeful than she had ever seen him before.

"You need to get moving now or the tunnels will flood. The rain is coming down hard. Just reme—"

A metallic clunk, like a kicked tin bucket, rang out as a grenade came bouncing into the centre of the cavern.

Instinctively, Sang leapt for cover, but rather than throwing fragments of burning metal across the room, the grenade flashed and started to smoke. A dizzyingly bright flare landed beside the canister, overpowering the dim glow of the lamps and illuminating the caverns with an ungodly red light, as though they had descended into the lowest level of the eighteen hells.

"Move. Now!" Captain Chien shouted.

"Blow the entrance," Sang yelled as she bolted down the southernmost path towards the river.

The old man clamped his remaining hand down on the pressure switch. He hit it hard enough that she heard the clack of metal on wood from twenty-five feet away.

Sang braced for the blast and the accompanying shock wave, but nothing happened. She spun her head around to see a look of disbelief in Chien's eyes. He clamped the switch again, adjusting the wires as he did, to no avail. Sang's stomach sank. The dampness of the cave infected everything. *Why didn't we think to check the charges?*

The former captain threw the switch down at his side and pulled his rifle to his shoulder, holding it in place with his stump. Without even a trace of feeling on his face, Huy followed Chien's lead and closed one eye, focusing beyond the flare light and down the tunnel.

Sang skidded to a halt on the damp stone beside the rope ladder. Grandma Lan, Khai, and Ly were still standing at the top of the precipice. "What the hell are you all doing here?"

"Ly wouldn't go," Khai answered. "She said we had to wait for you."

"You told me you wouldn't leave me," Ly sobbed.

Sang brushed her hair. "I'm sorry, darling, but we need to move right now. Understand? You *must* go down with Khai. I'm coming right behind you."

Ly sniffed and then settled into position with the boy's arm around her waist. The pair descended in unison, disappearing out of sight into the crevasse. Grandma Lan followed. The old woman looked surefooted but was way too slow even lowering herself down onto the top rungs of the ladder.

Sang ran back a few yards along the southern wall of the cavern towards the barracks, hoping not to draw the attackers to the river until their escape was assured. *I need to buy some time.*

Ducking behind a fossilised pillow of coral that swelled up from the ground like a massive porous hot-air balloon, Sang trained the barrel of her rifle on the entrance. She took a deep breath and waited. *I won't let them take anyone else from me. Not this time.*

Chapter Thirty-Five

Day Two
18:42
Fifty Years Ago

Flashes of white exploded from the tunnel, piercing through the haunting red glow that filled Sang's home. The deafening crack of gunshots bounced around the stone walls of the cavern like a thunderstorm in a box, drowning out the roar of rains from overhead and the rushing river.

Leaning around the bulbous, fossilised chunk of coral situated between her and the entrance, Sang squeezed the trigger, aiming blindly towards the attackers. Ares spat eight shots in the vague direction of the soldiers, momentarily halting the push as they adjusted their line of fire.

Under the cover of the smoke, it was impossible to tell how many of the Americans remained. Without the explosion to seal off the caves, it would make little difference in the end. Being overcome was all but inevitable.

Sang released another volley of seven shots and fell back, coughing and choking on the toxic fumes.

Bullets whistled and screamed around her, hammering into the rock she was using for cover. *Time to go.*

As Sang was preparing to make a dash towards the rope ladder, someone tossed a grenade out from behind the sandbags. The vast stone cavern groaned as a wave of noise and pressure crashed against the walls like breakers on a shore. Shards of metal followed, pinging off the rock on all sides.

With her head still spinning, Sang stumbled down the sloping pathway towards the river. Thirty feet from the edge, her foot caught a raised ridge of stone and her ankle folded under the immense pain.

The ground loomed towards Sang. Her forehead bounced off the wet stone and Ares slid from her grasp and skidded across the floor, coming to a stop halfway between her and the crevasse. Warm blood dribbled down Sang's face, clouding what little vision she still had left.

She scrambled back, taking cover behind an outcrop of stone. There was now just twenty feet of open space between her and the lip. Beyond it, the river, swollen by days of backed-up rainwater, was churning and swirling, faster and louder than she'd ever known it to before. They wouldn't have long until the underground tunnels were void of air completely, making any attempt at escape near suicidal.

The frayed top end of the rope ladder— hammered down with a railroad spike six feet from the edge—was scraping from side to side as Grandma Lan struggled on her way down. Sang doubted it would be able to take the weight of both of them. *Hurry up, damn you.*

In desperation, she glanced back over her shoulder towards the barracks, hoping against all odds to see her brothers-in-arms holding their own against the attackers.

The smoke had mostly cleared, trailing upwards to create a vast mustard-yellow cloud, as the light from the flare faded. Drops of rain showered down through the cracks above to complete the illusion of a hell storm raging inside the cavern.

Through the haze, Sang found the outline of Captain Chien lying face down near the centre of the cavern, missing half his head. She clenched her jaw, determined not to lose focus. Fortunately, Huy was still up there, sporadically firing over the top of the sandbags, fighting a losing battle. He caught Sang's eye and finally chose this moment to speak. "GO!"

Chapter Thirty-Six

Day Two

18:44

Present Day

A mist of blood and pus sprayed across Hector's back where he lay prone. He saw only the aftermath of the bullet that hit the one-armed soldier's face and killed him once again.

The idea that they could come in here and change something, somehow end the battle without complete death and destruction, seemed like a pipe dream at this point.

A cacophony of gunshots roared overhead. Hector's entire body flooded with adrenaline, heightening his senses and urging him to fight or flee. In a second's lull, he grabbed at Anna's wrist and yanked her towards him.

In a frantic half crawl, half sprint, they peeled off to the left, obscured by the smoke, towards the only cover he could see in the eerie, red-glowing cavern. The barracks.

As the shots started up again, Hector and Anna skidded down behind the metal shelter. Putting a barrier between them and the firefight, regardless of how flimsy it might be, was an immense relief.

The pair slipped around the rear of the structure until they could see the horseshoe-shaped fortification, ten feet to their right, backed into an alcove and protected on three sides.

A lone defender was behind the sandbags. The soldier's grey-skinned face was dripping with sweat and his torso was spotted with bullet holes, like a crimson polka dot shirt, but he didn't seem to have been hit, this time at least.

There was a gleam of madness in the man's eyes as he sprung up from behind the fortification, fired a quick burst of shots over the top, then dropped back down. He moved quickly from side to side, making his fire pattern unpredictable. All in all, the reanimated soldier was doing a valiant job of holding off the attackers.

Just as he ducked a third time, Em crashed into the sandbags. The model's long legs flailed momentarily in the air as her head and shoulders hit the ground on the far side.

Hector immediately second-guessed his decision of having chosen the flimsy tin wall over the thick, near-fossilised sandbag fortification. He turned back towards Anna. "We need to ge—Oh my God! What happened?"

Her face, lit by the glow of flare light, was tensed and twisted in pain. "I... I don't know," she said.

Anna was pressing both hands on her right hip as dark blood seeped out through her fingers. There didn't seem to be as much as Hector expected to see from a gunshot wound, but he was no doctor.

With an arm behind the small of Anna's back, Hector lowered her down against the wall of the barracks. She stared at her hands, covered in the dark liquid. "Am I going to die?" Her eyes were wide, her lips trembling.

"No. You're not." Hector held her gaze fiercely. "You're in shock. Just focus and we'll get through this," he said, trying to pretend he couldn't feel her body growing more and more limp by the second.

Hector ripped off his sleeve and covered her wound with it. His shirt was sweaty and disgusting, but preventing an infection was not his top priority right now. He wrapped the material over Anna's hip and looped it round under her left leg, tying it as tight as he could. It seemed to conceal the blood, at least. He prayed it would do as good a job at stopping the flow.

"Press down on this. We're gonna hide out here until they all kill each other, then make a break for it. We'll find something that floats, and I'll swim you back to the mainland."

In a moment of silence between shots, a child's wails and screams echoed up from the abyss and rang through the cavern.

Anna was crying, although whether it was from the pain or the sheer bleakness of their predicament was unclear. "Help them," she said. "I'll be okay."

Hector froze, wanting literally nothing less in the world than to leave her bleeding and run out to face almost certain death. "No. You need me. I'm staying here with you."

"Please."

"How?! I'm not a soldier. I'm a coward. Besides, everything I try just puts us in a worse position than before."

Anna gripped his hand and squeezed it tight. "You're not a coward, Hector. You can do this. I promise. We can't let those kids die again." The look in her eyes was one of utter desperation. "Someone needs to do the right thing. Just once."

From the corner of his eye, Hector caught a glimpse of Em quickly reloading a second Kalashnikov and swapping it with the bullet-riddled soldier who continued to lay down suppressing fire. It was a bizarre, yet strangely inspiring sight to see a reanimated corpse and a fashion model teamed up in a close-range gunfight. Although this dynamic clearly wouldn't last much longer.

The soldier screamed over his right shoulder to someone else hidden in the depths of the cavern. Hector followed his line of sight to the young woman who had thrown Anna the knife back in the forest. In doing so, she had certainly saved their lives. *The civilians are all still here. Damn it.*

He realised then that the defender wasn't even hoping to survive. He was just buying time for his people to escape. Did Em know? If he'd been wrong about her, he could have been wrong about himself too. Maybe he really could do this? One thing was for certain, he wasn't going to find out while hiding.

"I'll be back soon," Hector said to Anna. "Try not to move and, hopefully, you won't lose too much blood."

"Don't worry about me." She winced in pain. "I keep telling you, I'm tougher than I look. Now, go!"

Hector poked his head out from behind the hut. Rickard and Higgs floated across the cavern, a pair of ghosts in the fog, unloading a torrent of machine gun fire at anything that moved. A volley of bullets thudded into the damp sandbags, throwing off chunks of mouldy sodden dirt in all directions.

Em, who'd obviously had enough of playing soldier, was preparing herself for the ten-foot dash from the defences towards her friend behind the barracks. Just as she was about to run, a grenade flew over the top of the defences and landed behind her with a clunk.

The soldier didn't seem to hear the noise at all; he was busy returning fire. Meanwhile, Em was too distracted to even notice the device rolling around at their feet.

"Grenade!" Hector shouted, but amid the gunshots, his words were lost. *How long are the timers?* All he had to go off was playing Call of Duty. That gave him less than five seconds until they were all toast.

A wave of either bravado or foolishness, probably both, washed over Hector. He dived through the exposed gap over Em's head and landed hard, knocking the wind out of his lungs. His fingers fumbled for grip on the cold metal for what felt like far too long. Finally, he spun across his right shoulder, flinging the grenade back over the top like he was fielding a game of lethal cricket.

It blew in mid-air half a second later, throwing Higgs, who had been making a run for the sandbags, from his feet.

As Hector tried to recover his senses, stunned by the volume of the blast, Higgs was somehow already clawing himself back to his feet. A dozen shards of fragmented metal were lodged across his body and the peeling skin on his face was freshly seared. Instead of proving fatal, these wounds sent the soldier into a frenzy and he charged towards the defences, screaming with maniacal fury. *What the hell is this guy made of?*

The deaf soldier behind the sandbags, blissfully unaware of Higgs's death scream, turned towards Hector and gave him a thumbs up. Just as he did, four shots pounded into his chest.

At the same moment, Em reappeared sporting the second assault rifle and unloaded a burst of fire at their attacker. Higgs crashed into the ground three feet before the barrier.

She turned and grinned at Hector. "Pretty good for a—"

The young model's swollen neck exploded, coating his face with blood and sinew. Higgs, with his sidearm in hand, then finally slumped down dead.

Hector stumbled backwards, tripping over the deaf soldier and landed on the cold ground with his mouth agape. *I was wrong. I can't do this.*

Chapter Thirty-Seven

Day Two
19:02
Fifty Years Ago

Sang peered round the stone ledge and instantly locked eyes on her enemy. Rickard emerged from the smoke like a demon.

The sergeant, having noticed shots fired from the western side of the cavern, tracked his way smoothly down one of the paths towards the river. Working at a closer range on the lower level, he stowed his rifle over one shoulder and drew the same revolver that he had used to kill Long just a few hours before.

At the lip, Rickard peered down at the bloated river, but his angle made it impossible to see the tiny boat. Sang could still hear it clattering against the wall of the precipice. At this rate, escape would become completely impossible in a matter of minutes.

Sang glanced at the rope ladder to her left, straining and fraying under the pressure, on the verge of tearing itself free. The kids and Grandma Lan would be done for without her to steer the boat. Not one of them had the experience to do it themselves, especially in such furious waters.

Meanwhile, the American was ten yards from her position. Halfway between them lay Sang's rifle.

Something up by the barracks clattered, and Rickard swung round, taking aim at the shadows.

This was the opening Sang needed. To her left, Ly, the boat, and freedom. To her right, the man she owed a debt of blood. Her thoughts fell back to Truong, on his knees down by the river awaiting his death with honour, and a tremble of fury ran through her soul.

Sang bolted from behind her cover and dived for Ares. She hit the floor hard beside the gun but recovered fast. Sang pulled the butt up to her shoulder and took aim.

Moving faster than it seemed possible, the sergeant spun towards the noise, his revolver leading the way.

A searing agony exploded in Sang's shoulder. The .44 calibre round lodged into her clavicle, filling her face with smoke and her nose with the scent of her own burning flesh and bone. Ares slid from her grasp once again and this time disappeared over the edge.

Almost blacking out from the pain, Sang rolled onto her stomach and began to drag her bleeding body towards the ladder. In her exhausted, grief- and pain-stricken mind, a single thought cut through. *I promised Ly I wouldn't leave her.*

Just six feet from the abyss, a heavy army boot came stamping down on Sang's shoulder, pinning her to the ground. She seethed through her teeth and writhed in agony, not willing to give her enemy the triumph of a scream.

As if to complement her suffering, one side of the rope ladder tore free under the immense pressure. It left Ly, Khai, and Grandma Lan hanging on by merely a thread, facing an inevitable capsize when it went. Choking guilt overwhelmed all physical pain as Sang realised that her foolish desire to take revenge had doomed them all.

"You killed my men," the sergeant ground his heel further into her wound, cartilage and broken bone crunching against the floor. He drew a combat knife from his belt and spun the blade casually between his fingers. "Now, I'm gonna enjoy this."

As Rickard spoke, Sang slipped her free hand under her hip and silently wrapped her fingers around the hilt of the machete tied to her belt.

If her death was going to come at this bastard's hands, she was going to make sure she took him with her.

Chapter Thirty-Eight

Day Two
19:06
Present Day

A blinding rush of pain shot down Hector's right leg, reviving him from his daze. It took a few seconds to even realise why. A shard of sharpened metal, two inches long, poked out the back of his calf where it had been exposed to the grenade shrapnel.

Gripping the metal with oily fingers, Hector wrenched the fragment out, trying not to scream. Task accomplished, he stumbled to his feet, gritting his teeth through the pain, and took stock of the mayhem that surrounded him.

The smoke had started to dissipate, making the layout of the cavern less confusing at least.

Through the haze, Hector could see Rickard standing down by the river. He looked the literal incarnation of terror, looming over Sang with a foot on her shoulder, a gun in one hand, and his USMC blade in the other.

He glanced back towards Anna, who was still lucid, keeping pressure on her wound. Could she hold on for a few minutes longer? *She'll have to.*

Trying not to think about what would happen if he failed, Hector limped towards the river, crossing the centre of the cavern and sliding down a path near the entrance. Every instinct in his body was telling him not to go through with this. But in the midst of the crisis, a strange sense of calm washed over him. This was what he was meant for. He didn't know how to fight, fire a gun, or if he even could kill a man, but goddamn it, his words could be his weapons. He refused to be afraid any longer.

"STOP!" Hector yelled, skidding down the sloping path towards the two adversaries.

Rickard immediately swung the revolver towards him, keeping the girl in what would have been his peripheral vision if he had an eye. *Can he somehow still see her?*

Hector noticed Sang's hand wrapped around a machete in her belt, hidden from the sergeant's view by her torso. This was how it ended. In a few seconds, Rickard would stab her in the gut. Then, in a final act of revenge, Sang would punch a dozen vicious wounds into his groin and force his own gun into his eye. Unless, of course, Hector came out with something so compelling right now that these two mortal enemies would lay down their arms. That was a *very* tall order.

As Rickard honed in on the new threat, Hector raised his hands, but didn't stop his approach.

"You really don't know when to quit, do you?"

"I guess not."

"Well, you're a plucky motherfucker. I'll give you that. But why in God's name are you so invested in helping these gooks? What they ever do for you?"

"I'm not just trying to help them. I'm trying to help all of you. Because if I don't, nobody else will."

"What the hell are you talking about?"

"Can't you see what's happening here? This war is over. It finished half a century ago. Look at me. I talk differently, I'm dressed differently, I came here with a group of locals because we're not even enemies anymore!"

Hector held the sergeant's gaze. Rickard's forefinger was twitching on the trigger, but he chose not to fire.

"What's the year?" Hector continued. There was a hint of emotion in the sergeant's eyes, not just curiosity, but something else too… Fear. And fear was dangerous. He had to push harder. "When did you arrive on this island?"

Rickard thought for a moment. "Seventy-three," he said, suddenly sounding less certain. "We dropped behind enemy lines about two weeks back."

"Doesn't it feel like you've been here a lot longer than two weeks? Can't you remember anything else since?"

The look on the sergeant's pale, half-destroyed face showed the sheer depth of his confusion as he tried to cast his memories back. Then, all at once, it seemed to hit him like a brick.

"Now you come to mention it, I *do* remember this goddamn cave."

"That's good. What else?"

Rickard clenched his teeth, as if fighting through pain, forcing out memories like he was giving birth to them. "Nothing."

"Look at your eye then. Touch it. Can you see anything?"

Slowly, as though he'd just realised something was amiss, Rickard raised a hand to his face. His fingers made contact and he jerked back.

"You did this," he growled at Sang. "I remember it now. You stabbed me in the fucking balls, then put my last goddamn bullet through my eye!"

The sergeant flicked open the cylinder of his revolver to reveal a single shot left unfired. The very one destined to end his life.

Rickard's shoulders slumped. A very human look of sorrow spread across his deceased face. "It's always the same," he muttered.

"It doesn't have to be." Hector took a step towards him with his shaking palms raised, hoping the gesture looked friendly. "I know how we can end this hell you've been living for so long."

"How?"

"There are children down there." Hector nodded to the crevasse. "Don't kill the girl. Let us help them. Then maybe you can walk away with your life too. There must be someone you want to see again, a family, or something back home that makes all this worth fighting for?"

"My men *were* my family," he growled. "Anyone else I could have cared for, her people took from me. NO. STOLE FROM ME!"

Rickard spat suddenly, his mouth frothing with rage. As his heart rate picked up, the blood started pooling below him on the ground, dripping from where Sang was soon to brutalise his groin.

"You're lying, you fucking traitor!" Rickard snapped his head hard from side to side as if trying to shake himself from a nightmare. If there was one thing that made the sergeant even *more* dangerous than he would have been alive, it was the fact that he was hopelessly confused, his brain rotten and decayed.

"You're trying to get inside my head…" His voice swelled from a whisper to a shout. "I REMEMBER MY MISSION AND I WILL NOT FAIL. I *will* bring the wrath of God down on this island. Every last one of these motherfuckers will burn."

Rickard raised his gun and took a step towards Sang, who readied herself to finish this fight the same way it had happened so many times before.

Hector stepped in front of the sergeant's weapon.

"Get the fuck out of my way."

"I can prove what I'm saying is true."

The sergeant's remaining eyebrow raised. He wanted to believe there was an end to his suffering. "How?"

"Shoot me."

"This bullet is not meant for you."

"Stop being a pussy and do it!"

"Why? You're not one of them!" Rickard's face contorted in confusion.

"You've got one shot left, right? If that's the bullet that she puts in your head, then there's no way you can kill me with it. Just like my friend couldn't kill you. Either way, you win. Prove me wrong. Kill me. Then cut her throat. But if you can't, you have no choice but to accept the truth."

Hector took a step forward until the barrel was pressed against his forehead. The cold steel ready to prove his mortality. The sergeant gritted his teeth and fired.

Chapter Thirty-Nine

Day Two
19:14
Present Day

Dead?

Sang lay on cold, wet stone, her body screaming in pain. She'd hoped death would be more peaceful than this. *Fool,* she thought. *There was never any peace to be found here.*

Just as the shroud of despair engulfed her fully, a rattling at the bottom of the crevasse pulled Sang's groggy thoughts back from the edge.

In too much pain to even look back, Sang forced herself onto her belly and clawed, using her one still-working arm until she was peering down from the vertigo-inducing edge.

A second before she reached the drop, the remaining threads of the rope ladder finally tore free. She could do nothing but watch in horror as the tiny boat emerged from under the shadow of the cliff. It spun out to the centre of the river, teetering for a moment before flipping under the force of the current, sending three bodies crashing into the icy waters. *NO!*

A tiny pair of hands clasped onto the trailing ladder as it whipped and twisted through the water like a snake. By some miracle, one rung snagged upon a shard of rock in the centre of the flow. How long the little girl could last, fighting against the current and the weight of her heavy clothes, was a different matter altogether. *She still needs me.*

In a moment of desperation, Sang wrapped her fingers over the lip of damp stone and heaved her aching body forward until gravity claimed her.

Wind battered the young woman's face. She clenched her teeth and held her breath, knowing full well that it may be her last.

Sang's body shattered the surface like a falling stone. Tendrils of icy water clawed at her chest and the ravenous maw of the black river swallowed her body whole.

A curtain of blue gun smoke rose through the cavern, catching the remnants of the red flare light to create an eerie chemical cloud.

I'm alive.

Hector spun towards the young woman on the floor in a moment of elation. His joy turned to horror as she disappeared over the edge, taking any remaining hopes of success with her.

The splash a second later signalled Sang's descent into the furious waters. He dashed forward and peered down into the abyss, just in time to see a pair of bodies being washed away, both tangled in the remains of the torn ladder,

Could anyone survive that? Hector wouldn't have taken that bet. But if there was one thing he had learned from this entire ordeal, it was that people still had the power to surprise him.

He turned back to Rickard, who still had his gun raised, pointed at the space where Hector's head had been just moments before.

The sergeant's shoulders dropped. His lips moved as if speaking silent words. His expression was a mixture of shock, sorrow and, strangely, relief. Maybe he was glad? *God knows it must have been hard to live this once, let alone day-in-day-out for half a century.*

As if responding to Hector's thoughts, Rickard slumped down onto his knees. He placed the revolver on the ground in front of him and sighed as though suddenly it all made sense.

The sergeant turned his gaze up to Hector.

"I'm sorry... I really tried." Hector said, fighting back tears.

"Fifty years?" The sergeant shook his head in disbelief and stared down at the gun. "It's been far too long. They must have been waiting for me."

"Who must ha—"

Before he could finish his thought, Rickard snatched the weapon from the ground. Hector ducked on instinct, even though it made no sense that the sergeant would shoot him.

The two men's eyes locked for a fraction of a second. "No more waiting," he said, jammed the barrel into his eye and squeezed the trigger.

This time it fired. Sergeant Stanley Rickard was remortalised.

Chapter Forty

Day Two
19:23
Present Day

A hollow, soulless silence filled the void as the rushing river slowly eased back down to a steady flow. The screams and gunshots suddenly feeling like a thing of the distant past.

Hector tried his best not to look at the dead as he limped back past the sandbag fortification. Near the centre of the cavern, the one-handed older soldier lay face down. Higgs was slumped against the bags, while behind them Em and the deaf man were huddled together, almost like lovers in an embrace.

"Thank you," he whispered to Em as he passed. The young fashionista had given her life trying to free them. Even though she'd made some mistakes, Em had shown a selflessness and bravery he'd never have thought her capable of.

Behind the barracks, Anna was still breathing, although her face was sickly pale, almost looking like one of *them*. She smiled weakly at seeing Hector return, although she seemed delirious, giving him the impression she would have reacted the same with near enough anyone.

"You stopped them from dying?" she asked as he got closer, her voice cracking with pain.

I hope so.

"Yes," he answered. Right now, that was what she needed to hear. Truth be told, he did too.

Finding reserves of strength from somewhere, Hector lifted Anna with her arm over his shoulder and moved towards what looked like a supply cabinet in the corner.

Beside it sat a rusted, old weapons rack, and opposite, a wooden table, strewn with pieces of stone, dust, and decayed papers.

With one arm holding Anna up, he swept aside the junk on the table and gently sat her down on top. Among the rubbish he'd thrown across the floor, a tiny carved wooden doll caught his attention. Obviously, it had belonged to the little girl. Maybe it stemmed from Hector's misplaced sense of guilt, but the thought of leaving it behind stung. So he picked the figure up and slipped it into his pocket.

Hector searched through the cabinet and found a glass bottle. It was caked in half a century's worth of dust and mould as well as written in another language, but he was fairly sure it was alcohol. Beside it, there was a bundle of bandages, fortunately sealed in a brown paper packet.

"Brace yourself," he said, cracking the seal on the bottle.

Anna nodded in response, looking fearful. Hector wiped down the wound as she writhed and whimpered in pain. Then, he doused the bandages in the fluid, and wrapped the roll around her upper leg, covering her hip and tying it off around her waist.

Finally, the two survivors began a very long and slow crawl back out through the tunnel. This time, Hector barely noticed the insects, the dark, and the cold. The only thing that mattered was getting Anna to safety. He couldn't let anyone else die.

Six hours later, on the patch of dry ground at the southernmost tip of the island, Hector watched the sun rise. Anna lay asleep, her head cradled on his lap. He'd stayed awake, periodically checking her breathing. Fortunately, she really *was* much stronger than she looked. For that, he was thankful.

As the first rays of morning light spread out across the lake, Hector stared towards the water. He prayed Anna was right, and that he'd hear the chug of the boat returning a day late rather than the gunfire that signalled the start of the battle once again. For the next half an hour, they rested. Hector's breathing attuned to his companion's as she slumbered through pained, feverish sleep.

Then a low rumble echoed in the distance. He turned, following the noise as it skipped like a stone across the waters from the south.

BANG. For a moment Hector's dazed and sleep-deprived brain thought it was Rickard's shot.

Ten seconds later, the mint-green fishing boat chugged into view along the rocky shoreline, backfiring sporadically as it went. Hector watched the red flag on top of the shelter, growing closer. It billowed in the wind like the flame of a candle flickering atop a cake.

Overwhelming relief punched through the numbness. Tears streamed down Hector's face as the buck-toothed driver glided up to the lone patch of dry ground, waving from beneath his tin roof. Despite the fact that he was covered in fish guts, Hector had never been happier to see someone in his life.

As the boat approached, the driver's expression turned from a friendly grin to terror. He sped up and quickly threw a line out.

Hector grasped the rope as tight as he could manage in his exhausted hands while the fisherman pulled his boat in and leapt down, sporting a grim, knowing look.

Is he aware of what happens here? Hector doubted it, or he wouldn't have let Ricky, his friend, go in.

Hector tried to explain, but the driver quickly interrupted him, obviously not wanting to hang around any longer than was absolutely necessary. As they carried Anna up onto the boat, she stirred and mumbled, looking sick, injured, but undeniably alive.

Using as simple gestures as he could muster, Hector tried to explain that it was only the two of them left, and that Anna needed medical attention. This concept was certainly not lost in translation.

The driver wasted no time pushing away from the land with a barge pole, and held his thirty-year-old, back-firing engine at full throttle as they powered away, helped by the current.

The nearest patch of civilisation looked to be on the southern side of the lake, probably from where the fisherman had just come. Hopefully, they had a hospital.

As the small town loomed over the glimmering body of water, Hector held Anna's hand, hoping the rhythm of her pulse would stay steady. He glanced back over his shoulder at the fading silhouette of the island as they drifted away. *This can't have all been for nothing,* he told himself. *We must have made a difference.*

Chapter Forty-One

Day Three
04:48
Fifty Years Ago

Thick mud steamed around Sang as she lay face up on the bank. The warm light of a new day filtered down through the clouds, and a single ray spilled across her face.

Sweet, clean air swelled within her lungs. She coughed and convulsed, throwing up water. On instinct, she rolled onto her front.

Sang's icy fingers pierced the earth and found purchase. The mud sucked down her face and chest, as if refusing to release her from its death grip.

Where am I? The young woman's mind was foggy and dark. To pull any thoughts forward felt like trying to wade against the current of the river that had left her here. The tangled roots of the mangrove forest rose beside her on the left. To her right, a low muddy bank joined the lake a dozen yards further down.

The last thing Sang remembered was being pounded by torrents of rushing water, struggling for breath as she kicked her legs, gripping the tiny girl's arm—so small and weak—fighting to keep them both afloat. She recalled the exhaustion as it became overwhelming, and the current pulling her further and further down into the black.

Sang turned her head, looking towards the mountain behind her. That was when her eyes fell on the little girl lying just a few feet to the north. Ly's face was pale and her lips blue. Sang scrambled towards her and immediately began hammering down on the child's tiny chest, trying to force the water from her lungs.

Just as she was about to give up, Ly convulsed, retching a lungful of murky brown water out across the floor. The little girl coughed and spluttered. Her eyes flickered open.

Once again, Ly had returned from the dead.

Epilogue

In the few days that followed escaping the island, Hector and Anna were both moved from one rural hospital to the next. None of them seemed keen on taking responsibility for the pair of patients, despite Anna being stable and Hector's wounds being mostly superficial.

After questioning Hector in the hospital, the local police had jumped into action, sending a helicopter and a squad of officers to scour the island for the missing civilians. But two days of searching went by, with them finding nothing to corroborate his story, let alone four corpses.

Soon after, the local hospital sent Anna to Hanoi for treatment. Meanwhile, Hector was moved to a half-dilapidated old police station in the middle of nowhere.

The one staff member with decent English demanded he tell his story over and over, hoping to gain some clarity about what had actually taken place on the island.

After what felt like the hundredth repetition, Hector himself was starting to doubt his own sanity. Compounding this was the fact that no one had filed a missing person's report. Except for Ali, he didn't even know any of their full names, and the only descriptions he could give were so vague they could have been almost anybody.

He described the guest house where they'd all stayed in detail and several officers went to investigate, but apparently discovered nothing out of the ordinary. Hector begged them to let him go and talk to Van and see for himself, but his pleas fell on deaf ears.

Eventually, the senior officer determined that there wasn't anything more they could do. He assigned one of his men to accompany Hector and make sure he didn't run off. Then, after a full twenty-four hours on the road, they arrived at the psychiatric unit of a huge French-built hospital in downtown Hanoi.

Faced with the prospect of being committed to an asylum, Hector had no choice but to admit that he had made the story up. He claimed that he and Anna had found the gun and that it had gone off unexpectedly.

Although he didn't see her again, Anna apparently corroborated what Hector said because he was released a couple of days later with a nondescript bottle of pills and a diagnosis of extreme stress.

Rather than going straight to his embassy, as instructed, Hector immediately started looking into transport. He needed to get back to Van's guesthouse and find out one way or another if this was really all just in his head.

Unfortunately, with no money for tickets, no travel documents and the looming threat of jail time or being institutionalised, his plan soon hit a wall.

That afternoon, Hector tried a more low-key approach and found a gaming café where he could get online.

He looked up Ali on social media but found nothing remotely recent, as expected. He searched for Anna, but could only find Em, whose profile was filled with endless selfies.

However, there were a few photos of her and Anna from just over a week ago, documenting the trip right up until they first arrived at the guesthouse. But frustratingly, nothing since.

At a loss for what to do next, Hector started researching the island. With each minute that went by, he became more and more confident he hadn't just been imagining the whole ordeal.

Journalistic instincts possessed him and after a good four hours of reading through a cache of historical documents, he stumbled across a clue. On a government website, Hector found a death certificate for the commanding officer at the outpost. If he remembered Hoa's tale correctly, that must have been her brother.

More amazingly, it listed an address in the city where the document had been delivered, possibly a spouse or next of kin. This was a good place to start.

★ ★ ★

Despite being grey and overcast, the afternoon had been humid. Hector's clothes were still thick with sweat. Now, however, there was a touch of autumn-like coolness in the evening air.

From where he stood before the gates of an old and battered French colonial villa, Hector could see the lights on across the ground floor. There was a regal air to the structure, despite having obviously seen better days. Worm-holed wooden shutters with peeling green paint and soot stains covered the windows. On the dark upper floors, ornate patterned balconies and decorative brickwork jutted out. The whole thing was wrapped in a faded yellow jacket of ochre paint.

Above him, in the huge canopy of city trees, birds squawked at one another, calling their children home to roost. Somewhere at his rear, a motorbike honked, and a car alarm went off in response, making him jump. Hector's hands were still shaking when he pressed the rusted metal doorbell a full minute later.

After two minutes of waiting outside the wooden door, adorned with an iron mesh at the centre over a pane of glass, a teenage girl heaved it back.

"Hello?" she said with a strangely American twang, looking confused by the foreigner standing on the doorstep. She was maybe sixteen or seventeen, pretty, but had a friendly look about her.

"Oh. Hi." Hector suddenly realised that in all the madness, he had no idea what he wanted to ask. He wished he'd planned it beforehand.

"Is your mum or dad at home?"

"Yeah. MUM!" the girl called back over her shoulder.

A voice answered and there was a quick back and forth in Vietnamese as the mother approached.

Eventually, a middle-aged woman pulled the door back. She stuck her head out, taking a moment for her eyes to adjust to the gloomy evening light.

"Can I help you?" she said, switching to English.

"Yes." Hector's mouth was suddenly dry.

"Does a lady called Hoa live here? Or did someone called Truong ever live here?"

"No. This house was my mother's... I've lived here my whole life."

"Oh, okay," Hector replied, figuring he'd hit a dead-end.

Just then, a man—probably a husband—called something out from down the hallway, and the teenager shouted back. Half a dozen other voices started laughing, and the woman's face reddened slightly.

As Hector glanced towards the commotion, his eyes found a picture on the hallway wall behind the mother. *I know that woman.*

"Sorry, but I have to get back to my family," she replied, turning away.

"Wait," Hector said, raising a palm, and she paused.

"This is going to sound very weird, but do you recognise me?"

The teenager at her mother's side flicked out her phone and started filming their discussion, as though she instinctively knew it would be interesting.

"Sorry. I don't think so. Should I?" The woman's voice was friendly, maybe even a little amused by the bizarre line of questioning.

"Probably not, thinking about it." Hector thought for a moment. "One more thing."

"Yes."

"Is that a picture of your mother on the wall behind you?"

"Yes, why?"

"You were adopted, weren't you?"

The smile dropped off her face. She pushed her daughter's phone down, half-frozen in disbelief.

"Mum?"

The woman muttered something to her daughter in Vietnamese. With a shrug, the teenager disappeared into the depths of the house. A moment later, the laughter started again. Not mocking but happy laughter, a family together, enjoying one another's company.

The woman took a step forward, out onto the porch and pulled the door until it was just open a crack behind her. "I never told anyone that," she whispered. "How could you possibly know?"

Hector fished around in his pocket for a moment and pulled out what he was looking for. He held the small object up, pinched between his thumb and forefinger. "I believe this belongs to you."

The woman's hand was trembling as Hector laid the carved wooden doll in her palm. Tears were running down her cheeks. Her lips moved up and down as she tried to speak, and eventually she pulled out the words. "How did you know this was mine?"

"I've got a story to tell that you're not going to believe."

About *Remortalised*

Thank you for reading! I hope you have you enjoyed Remortalised.

I wrote this book as a culmination of real-life experiences (although fortunately, not with the living dead).

The first of which was a trip with my friend where we rode from Hanoi into Hoa Binh Province, and much like the characters, chartered a small boat to an island in the centre of the massive reservoir. This is also where the stories of the huge fish and many other details came from.

On this trip, we were setting up our tent on the island and were hit by an absolutely mighty summer storm (which, if you've never visited Southeast Asia, are usually of a truly epic scale). Our tent was promptly flooded, and we were forced to seek shelter under the eaves of a nearby stilt hut. However, things could easily have been overwhelming had we been a little further from civilisation.

The incident of Hoa searching for her brother's bones is based loosely on the stories from a journalist friend who lived in Vietnam for some time and interviewed a number of families about the process of searching for the lost victims of war.

Surprisingly, this is still a fairly common occurrence (even the necromancy), and although there are government programs set up to support the families of war victims, they are hugely under-funded. Furthermore, the task of locating the loved ones' remains grows more impossible with each year that passes.

As discussed in the book, it is also true that loved ones are traditionally buried, then exhumed after several years. The bones are then cleaned and prepared for cremation. Once, I had the honour of attending one of these rituals and found it both morbid and also extremely captivating. That said, had it been one of my family members, I would probably have felt differently.

The stories about the caves and the Ho Chi Minh supply trail walkers are all based on reality. In particular, the caves found in Cao Bang Province and Mai Chau, which served as storage and hiding places for the military supply routes during the Vietnam War and the Chinese invasion that followed.

The underground river and interior described is based directly upon the former of the two. I visited the location while doing research for a different novel that never came to fruition.

Similarly, the character of Sang was conceived for this same novel. I intended to have this book follow on from "Where Tigers Roam," a young adult martial arts novel set in the borderlands and mountainous ethnic communities of Southern China and northern Vietnam (a sample of this book follows), but my plans have since changed.

I searched for years for the right place to use Sang. Her identity is partially based upon real-life women, who will remain nameless for their (and my own) protection, but also on a number of stories of famous female militants during various conflicts throughout the latter nineteenth century.

Having lived in Vietnam for over a decade, I have often met women of the older generation who have shared harrowing stories of their roles and losses throughout the times of war.

Likewise, many of the military details and discussion of the tactics used, the environment, and various other elements come from the stories of my father-in-law, Toan. He was one of the supply troops that spent approximately three years walking the Ho Chi Minh trail and trying to avoid the constant artillery, bombers, and other dangers of the forest. He later worked as an AA gunner and became an officer. Toan has been extremely open about sharing many of his stories and never seemed to mind me asking bizarre details about his time on the trail (e.g. What is the weirdest animal you ever ate? Where did you sleep most nights?) There are so many of these stories that I couldn't possibly put them all into one story. Instead, I had to choose key details, such as the way they would disperse the smoke from their fires, sleep at a distance, and wear only rubber flip-flops. Therefore, my hope is that I did his and many others' stories justice.

I also intended to make this story as unbiased as possible, with "good" and "evil" characters on both sides of the conflict. I strongly believe there is no clear-cut "right" or "wrong" in times of war, particularly in the case of the Vietnam war, which was extremely complicated. Similarly, there are no victors, only victims.

Finally, I sincerely hope you have enjoyed reading *Remortalised*, and request that you please leave a review wherever you may have purchased this book. It truly makes all the difference for authors, and your comments would be greatly appreciated.

For more information, questions, or comments about my books, including fiction, non-fiction, and others, please follow me on social media or sign up to my mailing list at www.AJRoe.com.

Many thanks,
A.J. Roe

Keep reading for samples of the author's other works.

ABSOLUTION: A Legendary Adventure Thriller

1

"Let's turn back." Sanjay's voice was almost lost beneath the wind.

"Not yet. It'll be okay once we hit the beach." Rick Wilson *really* hoped he was right. A gale tore through the scrubby bushes and patches of long grass that spotted the desolate landscape as though it was desperate to uproot them. The sea air stung Rick's face, the salt burned his eyes and throat. Despite the thick green and black 'North Face' parka he wore over a jumper, long-sleeved shirt and T-shirt, a deep shiver lurched up from down below.

The past hour had been hell, but this was where Rick thrived. "A good man never gives up without a fight," his grandfather would often tell him as a child and he had taken those words to heart. If the stinging cold and ache in his legs were the costs for glory, they were ones he'd gladly pay.

With Sanjay just a step or two behind using him as an improvised windbreak, Rick quickened his pace, pressing forward down the steep grassy bank towards the icy Scottish sea. It was rising and falling in vast swells as though the Earth itself was huffing and panting beneath the surface. He glanced back to see Sanjay wearing the look on his face of a man who was seriously questioning his life choices. *He'll be fine.*

They trekked alongside the riverbank down to the water's edge for another thirty minutes. The grass of the open, windswept moors above slowly gave way to football-sized granite boulders and patches of black and grey shingle. They were slippery like ice under a mixture of sea spray, moss and clumps of seaweed.

Soon enough, the pair reached a row of towering cliffs that jutted out from the shore. The vast chunks of granite offered a slight respite from the howling, icy wind. *Damn, I hope the crazy old bastard was right.*

Rick tucked himself in against the cliff face and swung the heavy backpack from his shoulders. He dropped it to the ground, not giving a second thought to the equipment inside, which had already been thoroughly battered over the years. In a squat, he sat with his back against the stone and the heels of his leather hiking boots dug into the shingle.

Sanjay slid down to his right, a look of distinct displeasure on his face. "I can't believe I'm giving up my weekend for this," he said, fighting to be heard over the roar of the wind.

"Look on the bright side, man. The Scottish Moors is one to tick off the bucket list."

"Yeah, well at least now I know not to bother coming back."

Rick stifled a smile. As they rested, he scanned the horizon in both directions and something caught his eye. "Look." To the east, a mile or so away, the crumbling first and second floors of a mansion were clinging to life over a half-collapsed cliff edge. It was almost obscured by a closer outcrop, from any other angle or up on the clifftop, the decrepit structure would have been completely invisible. "I can't believe we didn't see it before. It's exactly as he said."

"True," Sanjay replied, "but this whole coast is covered in dilapidated buildings. Personally, I'm still not convinced by the stories of an old drunkard you met in the pub."

"Pfft. Come on, let's get moving, you'll see." Rick prayed he was right, with the number of hours of his life that had gone into combing through archaic shipping manifests and pages of old diaries, there was no way he could give up now, he was in way too deep.

Plenty of anecdotal evidence supported the historical records; four hundred thousand pieces of

Spanish gold, in seven chests, *had* arrived on this coastline in 1745. Of the seven, four had been accounted for and eventually arrived with their intended recipients, but another three had mysteriously vanished into the ether.

Through a mixture of official and unofficial references, the disappearance of these three chests could be pinned down to a very specific geographical area. Although they certainly weren't the first to come searching here, Rick had one thing all the others didn't, desperation.

At this rate, in less than two months he'd be bankrupt. If that happened then he wouldn't even be allowed to see his daughter, let alone try to rebuild some kind of relationship with her.

With almost insurmountable effort, Rick pushed off the wall with his back, willing his cramping thighs back into action.

By mid-morning, the wind had begun to soften and a sliver of sunlight pierced through the blanket of grey overhead. This made the miserable trudge on tired feet and with aching knees from the uneven ground, slightly more bearable.

Rick and Sanjay worked west along the wet shingle, weaving around vast granite pillars. Stripes of barnacles and seaweed, almost at head height, on their surfaces indicated two things. One: that the tide was abnormally low, and two: that it would soon be on its way back in.

A good twenty minutes passed before their route was blocked by a larger outcrop than the others, it jutted from the coastline far out into the low, late summer tides. Rick eyed up the water around its body, frothing and foaming, swirling and smashing against the rock. There was no way of telling how deep the drop off into the frigid sea would be.

Rick turned on his heels, studying their surroundings for a sign to confirm his suspicions. The monolith ahead had a thick build-up of brown kelp across its face, revealing just how rare it was that the waters receded so far. "This is it. It must be."

Everything that Rick had read indicated a tidal cave on the Southwestern Scottish coast that met a very specific set of criteria. It had to sit at the foot of a river which doubles a full one-hundred-eighty degrees back on itself before it reaches the sea but was also within viewing distance from the windows of a nearby clifftop estate.

Rick had waited months to visit until the tides were at the lowest point of the year. He had pinned down three promising locations, all within striking distance to be done over the long weekend.

Saturday had been a bust; they'd searched the most likely area for an entire day but got nothing for their troubles. All of their maps were near enough useless too, with the constant cliff-falls and fast eroding coastline, there wasn't a single recognisable landmark or defining feature to be found.

Rick was beginning to understand just why this vast fortune had stayed lost for so long and the stress of impending failure was weighing heavily on his shoulders. That evening, while Sanjay had caught up on sleep, Rick went for a well-needed treble of the local single malt in one of the two pubs in the tiny town of Abury.

By sheer luck he had got talking to a half-cut descendant of some local clan about what they were doing in the highlands. The old man was stocky and unkempt but his eyes had a look of experience in them that was hard to ignore.

Rick listened intently as the clansman rambled on, in an accent almost as thick as his beard. While the slurring old man's theory about how the treasure had disappeared was all wrong, he described a location that sounded suspiciously like the last site on their list.

This is it, Rick told himself as though it might make it true. Sanjay was already scanning the walls of the pillar close to the sea's edge. The bottom ten feet of the massive stone outcrop would all usually be well below sea level, even during low tides, but today the waters were raked back leaving it fully exposed.

Sanjay worked methodically up and down, running his hands across the surface. He was one of the most experienced and knowledgeable men Rick knew, with a working understanding of everything from geology to particle physics. Unfortunately, Sanjay was also the type of man who preferred theory to field work, happy to be in the lab or the library, the polar opposite of himself.

As they crawled up and down, probing every crack and crevice, Rick's hopes of glory began to fade. He wasn't often let down by his hunches. "Let's break for lunch," he called out after half an hour or so and began to drag his legs, like dead weights, back towards the shelter of the cliffs.

"Wait!" Sanjay shouted back, "Come here." The excitement in his voice was palpable. Rick swung around to see him lying face up on the shingle, reaching his hands upwards, his fingers probing some kind of space beneath an overhang of rock a few feet from the frothing waves.

"What is it?"

"Give me a torch. It looks like it opens up under here."

Rick's frozen hands fumbled with the straps of his red Petzl climbing backpack. After a minute or so, he found one of the two powerful LED torches he'd packed. He placed it into Sanjay's open palm and stood over his friend bobbing up and down on the balls of his feet for some of the longest seconds of his life.

"It's a cavern." Between the wall of rock and wind, Sanjay's voice was all but lost.

A few seconds later the academic pushed his body out from beneath the crag, revealing a Cheshire Cat grin, his white teeth shining like pearls. "What are you waiting for then? Get in there."

As Sanjay pulled himself to his feet, Rick smacked him across his wide back with a solid open palm. "You're a legend mate!"

Throwing his backpack down onto the wet rocks and rummaging through it. Rick pulled out a half-inch-wide red and grey nylon climbing rope. He tied a triple bowline knot giving a loop for each leg and one for his waist, a pretty solid improvised harness.

After double checking all of the knots—knowing a well-tied rope could mean the difference between life and death if things went badly—Rick climbed in and passed Sanjay one end. He slid beneath the overhang and clicked the button on his torch. Aiming the beam upwards at the slimy mottled walls, Rick took in a sight that would change everything.

You can purchase "Absolution: A Legendary Adventure Thriller" from all major retailers.

Acknowledgements

For their support with writing, editing and designing this book, I would like to thank Le Thanh Ha, Le Huy Toan, Ann Roe, David Bell, Andie Edwards at 'Beyond The Proof' and all the early draft readers who helped me pin down the plot and content.